THE
MAN
IN THE ELEVATOR
ROXANA NASTASE

Scarlet Leaf

2018

PUBLISHED BY SCARLET LEAF

Toronto, Canada

Table of Contents

TO MIRCEA, A FUNNY, JOLLY MAN

CHAPTER ZERO

H is hands stuffed in the pants pockets, Dan entered the elevator, whistling softly. The man felt good. He had just picked up the new girl who started working on the fourth floor a week ago. Now, he already had a date lined up.

'*Great rack,*' the man thought and arched his left eyebrow admiringly. '*And those pouting lips,*' he shook his head and swallowed hard.

The young woman embodied everything he enjoyed most in a female, and he couldn't wait to score.

He didn't do that just to add a new notch over his bed. He genuinely loved women, regardless the color of their hair or eyes. His standards were high only when it came to the size of their bust and lips.

The doors slid silently and closed. Then, the elevator started the slow trip up to the seventh floor.

'*You can count on just a few things in this lifetime,*' the man shook his head in dismay and brushed his fingers through his dark hair with anxious gestures. '*Taxes, death and slow elevators. Damn, I'll be late again, and they'll have my head soon enough if I keep coming late from my break,*' he reflected with a frown and shoved his hands into the pockets again.

His last meeting with the supervisor hadn't gone to well. He had him sign a formal notice. If he was late again, Dan would have lost an hour from his pay, and every penny counted when he had to wine and dine beautiful women.

The elevator slowed down when it reached the third floor, and the doors slid open with a quiet woof. Dan grimaced for a second, but then the man plastered a smile on his lips.

'*You never know who you might encounter,*' he thought sagely. It wouldn't do to get on someone's wrong side merely because the elevator annoyed him.

A few seconds later, Dan's smile froze on his lips, and his hands clenched in tight fists.

CHAPTER ONE

"Come on, Liza, you must be joking, girl," Ana-Maria replied loudly, bursting into laughter, and eyeing her friend askance. "I can't believe that Dan really did that. What the heck? Is he out of his mind?"

Ana-Maria balanced the paper coffee cup and the sandwich she was holding in one hand and pushed the elevator button with the other. A lock of light-brown hair teased her face, and she brushed it nervously behind her ears. Her hazel eyes sparkled with curiosity and measured Liza again. Her colleague was well-known for her talent to embellish things, after all.

"I'm serious, really," Liza nodded. "I mean I wasn't there or anything like that, but Dana was, and she swears that she spoke the truth," the redhead said in earnest, and her green eyes glanced at the elevator lights again.

Exhausted from carrying all those snacks in her hand, Liza leaned on the wall by the elevator. '*What the heck made me offer to go and buy snacks for five other people?*' the young woman scolded herself.

"I can't believe it," Ana-Maria shook her head in bewilderment. "I knew that he was a bit crazy, but that's way over the top. Really? Did he actually take off his clothes in the middle of the club?"

"Yep, he did. Of course, he was dancing on a table right then," Liza nodded and looked at the elevators around to see if any would come.

'If I counted the minutes I've spent before these closed elevator doors, I would probably discover that at least ten percent of my life has been wasted just looking at these blasted lights,' she sighed inwardly.

"But I can't believe that the club enforcers didn't react to something like that at all," Ana-Maria shook her head, laughing.

"They did, all right," Liza replied. "You see, this time, Dan went way too far, and they banned him from the club. For good."

"That's the fourth one by now, I think," Ana-Maria tilted her head inquiringly.

"I can't say I have kept count," Liza shrugged. "It's not like I care too much about what happens to him, you know," she said in a hard tone of voice.

'You care all right,' Ana-Maria thought with malice.

She knew that Liza had been in love with Dan for quite a while. The two of them dated for some time, but the man didn't seem to think about her anymore.

In fact, Dan liked diversity. Ana-Maria had been working together with him in the same place for about three years now. Until then, she had seen him with another woman at least every other month.

THE MAN IN THE ELEVATOR

Liza had made a mistake getting involved with him. But then, she had nurtured the hope that the man would change.

'Frequent mistake among women, from what I could see,' Ana-Maria reflected with an inward shrug. She had done it herself in the past and hoped to have learned her lesson.

"Finally, it's coming," Liza noticed with a sigh of relief when the light of the elevator blinked.

The doors opened, and the young woman started forward. Her eyes fell on the body on the floor and practically popped out of their sockets. An ear-splitting scream burst out of her throat, and Ana-Maria stepped back, scared of her friend's behavior. Still, she tilted her head to look past Liza. A second later, she leaned on the wall. Her legs shook, and the blood left her face.

The young woman watched her coffee cup spill on the hallway floor, followed by the sandwich. She hadn't even realized that she had dropped everything she had in her hands. But then, she didn't feel her fingers anymore.

Liza continued screaming the building down, and both of the security men from the front desk ran toward them to see what the matter was. The older one passed by Ana-Maria, and his eyes swept over her in a split second. The younger followed him, on the edge, ready to react. First, their eyes fell on Liza, who continued screaming like a banshee.

'She's got good lungs on her, this one,' the older security guard thought and shook his head.

When he looked past her, and his eyes fell on the man on the floor, his jaw twitched, and his eyes turned hard. *'Yep, this workday isn't getting any better,'* he thought morosely.

"Come with me," the man said gently, grabbing Liza's arm and steering her out of the elevator. "Call the police," he threw over the shoulder toward his younger colleague. "I'll take the ladies to the lounge. Block this elevator and don't let anyone get too close for a look," he warned the man in a confident tone of voice.

'*As if I had had more experience than he does,*' the old man scoffed inwardly and shook his head again.

He had been working as a security guard for over fifteen years. That was true. But then, that was his first encounter with a crime scene. He sincerely hoped it would be the last.

"*Thank God for all those crime show series,*" he reflected, showing the two shocked young women toward the lounge.

CHAPTER TWO

A lex Pop strode into the building with long steps. He had shoved his hands into the coat pockets, and a grey hat covered his forehead and his eyes. The man stopped in the middle of the lobby, and his eyebrows shot up his forehead in bewilderment.

The front desk appeared to be deserted, although the annoying ringing of a phone pierced the silence. The man looked around for a few moments and then tilted his head to the right. He had the feeling that he had seen some movement somewhere above the four steps leading to the turnstiles.

Pop wasn't wrong. Three security men stood in the area of the elevators, talking quietly among themselves and gesticulating.

Suddenly, the door of an elevator on the right opened, and a group of five people exited the cabin. Curiosity took the best of them, and they tried to see beyond the three men who blocked the way to the elevator in the back.

"Move along, people," the older security guy waved them ahead. "Nothing to see here," he pointed out, bad-mugging them.

Hesitantly, the people moseyed toward the turnstile, whispering among themselves. Afterward, they passed by Pop and measured him with light bafflement.

A grin tugged at Pop's mouth. He knew that his presence in the building would raise eyebrows. Most of the people in such companies dressed in blue jeans and sneakers, while he usually sported black trousers, a coat and overcoat. Besides, his soft hat would always make people comment, but he didn't really care.

Pop was a non-conformist. It had been quite a while since he paid attention to people's opinions. He preferred feeling comfortable in his own skin and projecting a certain image. If the others didn't appreciate the way he dressed and behaved, that wasn't his concern.

He dressed either like that or in his leather suit if he rode his motorcycle. This time, he had to come directly from the courthouse, and judges didn't really appreciate detectives who looked like a gang leader. They used to frown upon such appearances.

Pop stepped aside to let the group of people go out and then strode toward the turnstiles.

"I understand you're in need of the police," he said to the security guards in a dry tone of voice.

The people turned to him at once and measured him with various expressions on their faces. Pop merely arched his right eyebrow and tilted his head questioningly, inviting them to confirm or deny his words.

"And you are?" the older security guard replied after measuring openly the man with the funny hat.

"The police," Pop replied very matter-of-factly. "Or part of it," he corrected himself. "The others are on their way," the man added, glancing at his watch.

As a matter of fact, he had a head start because the others had been retained. The forensic experts had been called to another case earlier, and the coroner had let him know that he was just in the middle of a post-mortem and could come only after about thirty or forty minutes later.

"I see," the security guard murmured, although he didn't seem very convinced of Pop's words. "Do you have an ID or something?" the man inquired, unwilling to allow any nosy guy to take a look at the crime scene. He even wondered if the guy with the hat wasn't actually a reporter. '*Nowadays, you never know what else they will make up just to grab a subject,*" the man reflected.

Pop glanced at him sideways but then took his ID out of his coat pocket and showed it to the man, who took care to verify it minutely.

"Yes, you're the police," the old man acknowledged, and not without bewilderment. "Geo, go and let the man pass," he waved to one of the younger guards. "Go there, sir," he indicated to Pop, pointing toward the front desk where Geo had already run and lifted a bar to allow the policeman to come into the secured area of the building.

Pop took his sweet time to get to the front desk. The man didn't see any reason to hurry right then. Anyway, he couldn't do anything before the coroner and the forensic experts came. He had enough time to take a look at the body.

He passed by the young security guard and read the man's name on his badge tag. '*Another Popescu,*' he reflected. '*This city is overpopulated with Popescus, Ionescus, Pops and Georgescus,*' he concluded.

He would have liked not to get lost in the sea of anonymity of the popular Pop, but fate had dictated things differently.

Pop nodded toward the young Popescu gravely. '*One must keep a certain dignity on the job,*' he thought, although he didn't give a fig about such things.

However, he still remembered the Police Chief-Commissioner's admonishment about his lack of professionalism in certain situations. '*Apparently, smiles aren't allowed on the job, man, so I'm sorry, but I can't get too friendly with you,*' Pop addressed the young guard in his mind.

The policeman wasn't a very talkative man - outwardly. Yet, he had full conversations with himself and the people around in his mind.

Pop strode slowly toward the other two security guards who hadn't left the area with the elevators.

"Considering your position here, I think that the body is in one of the elevators," he said.

"Yes, sir, right there," the old man pointed out the elevator in question to him.

Pop nodded and his eyes stole to the man's badge. The detective in him didn't allow him to deal with unknown people.

'*I was right again,*' he mused. '*This is another Georgescu,*' he concluded after he read the man's name.

THE MAN IN THE ELEVATOR

"Mr. Georgescu, I presume," he stretched his hand toward the man. '*I don't think that shaking his hand means that I am too friendly,*' he thought, assessing the man's face at the same time. '*Or at least, that's what I hope,*' he corrected himself.

The old man shook the policeman's hand after a brief hesitation. His eyes had rounded in surprise because he hadn't expected the man to do that. The detective seemed too aloof to show such a courtesy.

"Yes, sir, I'm Georgescu," the man said, and he looked meaningfully down toward his badge.

"I'm Police Inspector Alex Pop," the officer introduced himself. "Now, let's see that body. Any idea what happened?" he asked.

"Not really," Georgescu replied. "We know only that two young women wanted to go into the elevator and found the body. They screamed the building down, and we rushed to see what had happened and found him like that," the old man pointed to the body lying on the floor.

All the snacks Liza had held in her hand had scattered around, and the pool left by Ana-Maria's spilled coffee flirted with the edge of the cabin.

Pop's eyes swept over the food and then over the body lying on the spotted floor of the elevator. Blood had flown freely, sign that probably an artery had been hit. It had already coagulated on the wooden surface.

The victim seemed young enough, maybe not even thirty-five. He had been a strapping man with a full head of thick dark hair. His eyes had widened, as a result of the shock, and Pop concluded that either the man had been taken by surprise or he had known his murderer.

The Police Inspector looked around but wasn't able to spot the murder weapon. *'If it hasn't ended up under the victim, the killer took it with him,'* he concluded.

The Inspector's fingers itched to search under the body, however he couldn't. Until the coroner came, he couldn't do a damn thing and was there just like a mere puppet, looking around and pretending that he was busy and in the process of very important deductions.

"You said something about some women," he turned his eyes toward Georgescu, arching his right eyebrow inquiringly.

"Oh, yes, indeed. The young women who found him here," the security guard nodded wisely. "They wanted to get back to their floor, and when the elevator doors opened, the view shocked them. All the food and coffee on the floor belong to them," he thought to mention.

"I can understand why they were shocked," Pop replied. "Still, where are they now?" he asked.

"Oh, they are back in the office. I thought of separating them, but one of them was beyond shocked, and we needed the other woman to calm her down because she had become hysterical. I have the feeling that her acquaintance with the victim went a little deeper than just a mere fellowship. Both women seemed to know him. They work on the same floor with him, after all."

Pop nodded and opened his mouth, wanting to ask them to lead him to the back office, but he didn't have the time. Sirens sounded very close to the front door, and everyone turned their head that way.

CHAPTER THREE

Sirens weren't out of place in the area. With at least four hospitals in the vicinity, sirens blasted all the time, regardless of the time of day or night. People either learned to live with them or moved out.

The forensic team led the way into the building, followed by the coroner and the prosecutor, who were chatting quietly between themselves, careful not to be overheard. When the prosecutor laid his eyes on Alex Pop, a smile fleeted on the man's lips.

Pop had already become a very well-known character in the police force of the capital, and not only because of his controversial career. The man had lots of idiosyncrasies, and his extreme attitudes and actions succeeded in raising his Chief-Commissioner's hair up. Rare were the cases when the man didn't do something stunning.

A lone wolf, Alex Pop didn't really socialize with anyone. He kept to himself, and his colleagues didn't know how he spent his time outside his work hours, although people advanced various outlandish hypotheses regularly.

In spite of his reclusive personal life, most of the people liked him well enough, and the coroner and prosecutor were part of that group. The detective showed a sharp sense of justice and very strong work ethic, which made his colleagues either admire him or loathe his presence with a vengeance.

Nonetheless, the man didn't seem to give a fig that he had divided the people at the headquarters in two camps. He just cruised through his daily life without a thought for what the others whispered behind him.

When he saw the two men, Alex Pop hesitated for a second but then decided to welcome them. He stepped forward, eyeing both the coroner and the prosecutor with a critical eye.

In fact, both men, at least a decade older than Pop, had always represented a role model for him. The detective had heard about several difficult cases the two of them had solved in the company of Pop's Chief-Commissioner, George Baranga, and even researched them.

The prosecutor, Paul Burada, a man well over forty, wore his baldness with pride. The man shaved his head and refused obstinately to join the hordes of men who tried to cover their skulls with a longer lock of hair. He knew that the slightest whirl of wind would have easily dislodged it from its spot, and he could live just fine without the ridicule.

A former boxer, Burada filled his clothes well, and whenever he made a sudden move, people would cringe with fear. More than just a few expected that the seams of his coat or trousers would give way.

The man's olive green eyes betrayed his shrewdness, but also the fact that he had seen quite enough things in his lifetime, and very little could surprise him anymore.

THE MAN IN THE ELEVATOR

Everyone knew that Burada and the coroner, Victor Danila, shared a lifelong friendship. They had met in grade school, and their relationship withstood the test of time.

Both of them showed utter indifference to the impression they left on the people around. That didn't mean that they hadn't noticed the coy smiles which appeared on people's faces whenever they spotted the two of them together.

The coroner was in the possession of a full head of curly grey hair, and not just a few individuals envied him for that. However, he always looked like an unmade bed as if he had never had the time to run a comb through his rebellious curls.

Burada towered over Danila, and he weighed at least one hundred fifty pounds more than his friend. Quite a few fellows remembered what a joker had once said, *"In case of danger, Burada could easily pick up Danila under his arm and run with him for shelter."*

"A new case, hmm," the prosecutor observed, shaking the Inspector's hand.

Pop just nodded, and then shook the coroner's hand as well.

"Lead the way, lad," Danila invited him with a wave of his hand.

"Do we know what happened here?" Burada chimed in, turning on his heel and following Danila and Pop toward the front desk to pass toward the elevators.

"Not as of yet. I just saw the body, and besides the fact that there is a lot of blood, I didn't see too much, to be honest. I didn't want to disturb the crime scene before the forensic team and the coroner came," Pop confessed with a nonchalant shrug.

"Good thinking, lad," the medical examiner thumped him on the shoulder, a grin tugging at the corners of his mouth. "Let's have a look, then," he started forward, leading the pack with the purposeful steps of a man who knew his job.

As a matter of fact, the Inspector always admired the doctor's confidence and often thought to emulate him.

Alex Pop and the prosecutor followed the doctor a few steps behind, unwilling to get in his way. The security guards also stepped aside, intimidated by the bearing of the shorter man. A couple of them even brushed against the wall behind them.

"Too many people around here," Danila said in a hard tone of voice. "I'm sure that we will do just fine with only one of you," he informed the guards. "You probably have other things to do, don't you?" he concluded with obvious sarcasm.

The man was known for a lot of things. However, tactfulness wasn't one of them.

The guards swallowed hard but nodded and left the area. Only the older security guard remained, his eyes following the doctor's moves attentively, as if he had feared that the man would steal something.

Georgescu had suddenly developed a strong dislike for the man and looked avidly to find something that he could reproach to him. '*I'm the boss around here, after all,*' he scolded himself for his initial shyness.

The medical examiner didn't bother to read the man's expression. He rarely cared about what the people he encountered thought.

THE MAN IN THE ELEVATOR

The man stopped before the elevator first, and his shrewd eyes swept over the scene carefully. His pupils followed the direction of the blood flow and the splatter on the side of the elevator cabin. Then, his eyes trailed over the victim's face, from the shocked expression in his open eyes to the painful and frozen grimace, which curved the corners of his mouth downward.

The coroner shook his head knowingly. He didn't doubt that the man had had the shock of his life when he had made the acquaintance of a sharp blade, which a strong hand had savagely shoved into his lower abdomen.

Danila didn't hurry to start a closer examination. Burada and Pop waited patiently behind him, aware that the doctor had his own habits when it came to such examinations.

Georgescu frowned, and his thick eyebrows bunched together. '*What the heck is he doing? Does he mean to revive the body just by looking at it?*' he reflected sarcastically.

Unaware of the man's thoughts, Danila finally put his medical bag on the floor and opened it, taking a pair of surgical gloves out of it. Then, he hunched next to the body and started his close exam.

Silence was so thick that it permeated the air. Suddenly, the doors of an elevator opened with a muffled whoosh, and Georgescu practically jumped out of his skin. He was so focused on the doctor's measured gestures that he had spaced out. The man bit his lower lip to muffle a scream and then looked around guiltily.

Burada grinned knowingly and elbowed Pop without taking the care not to be seen. Pop just shrugged and shook his head, but the security guard still turned scarlet.

"I don't think that you need me anymore," the man mumbled to no one in particular. "I have other things to do. The two women who found the body are in the back office there with one of my men," he thought to mention, pointing into the general direction of the door toward the stairs.

"Thank you," Pop replied in a quiet tone of voice. "We'll talk to them in a minute," he added and thanked the man with a nod.

Georgescu left mumbling under his beard, and Burada's grin grew wider. He didn't hear the man's words, but he had enough imagination to know that the guard didn't express any kind thoughts about them.

"The guy was done in with one blow to his spleen," the medical examiner concluded. "The blade encountered an artery, as you can see from the jet of blood that got to that corner of the elevator. I imagine the murderer has been splashed as well, considering the void here in the trace of blood," the doctor showed to them. "It would be interesting to find out how he or she vanished," the doctor mused, biting his lower lip. "He'd have been seen at least by the security guards if he had left the building that way," he pointed toward the turnstile. "A person covered in blood would have drawn everyone's eyes," the man affirmed with conviction.

"I'll check to see what security measures are in place for the access onto the floors upstairs," Pop observed quietly. "And of course, I will also check if there isn't any other way to go out of the building," he rushed to add when he noticed that the prosecutor wanted to intervene.

Indeed, Burada had wanted to infer the existence of an alternative exit, and he nodded, delighted with the Inspector's train of thought.

"Maybe you should check the security guards as well," Danila couldn't keep his mouth shut and chimed in maliciously. "Who knows, they might have had an understanding with the murderer," he added, winking toward Burada.

"I doubt that," Alex Pop shook his head, without feeling any restraint to contradict the doctor.

The officer respected the man, but he had an inkling that the doctor was just pulling his leg. That theory rang too phantasmagoric to even think about it.

The metropolis might have known one or two cases of murder conspiracies along the last few decades, but the policeman found that he had a hard time to place Georgescu, the older security guard, in the position of a co-conspirator. The guy rather looked like a man who impatiently counted the years he had left until he could retire and fill his days with only taking care of his tomatoes or cabbages.

Despite the old man's obvious impatience to take his place in the world as a retired senior, Pop couldn't believe that Georgescu would have turned a blind eye when it came to murder. The man might have looked the other way if someone had left the building with a toilet paper roll stashed inside their bag, but a murder was a far cry from that.

Danila's lips twitched with mirth. As he expected, Pop hadn't understood that he had merely joked with him. '*The boy takes everything too literally*,' the coroner mused and shoved the surgical gloves into the bag proffered by one of the forensic examiners.

"Well, you don't need me here anymore, lad," he thumped Pop over the shoulder. "I have a hot date in town with Mrs. Danila for lunch, and you can't imagine how vocal she can become if I am late," he mentioned, stealing a look at his watch. "And I'll definitely be late this time," he shook his head ruefully. "Eh, I'll choke my food down," the doctor shrugged with resignation.

However, he didn't understand how it was possible for his better half not to have come to terms with the rigors of his work after so many years. His wife was stubborn but smart enough to grasp even more complex concepts.

"I'm sure that Alex is capable enough to see to the investigation here by himself," Burada said, looking steadily into the young man's eyes.

Alex Pop nodded seriously, and the prosecutor grinned.

"Then, I'm off, too," the man said. "I'll let your boss know that I gave you free rein in dealing with the interviews. You'll bring me up to speed tomorrow morning," the prosecutor said and shook the Inspector's hand, taking his leave.

Danila and Burada left together, and Pop followed their departure with circumspect eyes. He remembered well the Chief-Commissioner's comment at the conclusion of his last case and expected that the prosecutor would return any moment.

THE MAN IN THE ELEVATOR

His boss had blown his gasket when he found out that Pop had solved the case by infiltrating a gang and posing as an aspiring member. Before that, the Inspector had gone through several sessions of hard drinking with a couple of the gang members.

The problem had been that he hadn't asked for any authorization to do that, and implicitly, he hadn't had any back-up with him. If anything had happened to him, no one would have known until it had been too late.

George Baranga, Pop's Chief-Commissioner represented the quintessence of tact and hardly if ever admonished a subordinate in other people's presence. Yet, at that time, the man had been mad like a bull and made that comment right in front of Burada's amused eyes.

Pop had a hard time believing that the prosecutor had forgotten about it. Pop wasn't supposed to lead any investigation by himself anymore. Baranga had decreed that the officer needed a shadow all the time.

When Burada stopped a taxi and left, Pop's eyes filled with puzzlement. He had half expected the prosecutor to return after he exchanged a few words with the doctor.

Pop shrugged and glanced at the forensic experts, who were hard at work. Then, the man turned around and looked for Georgescu at the front desk, but the old man wasn't anywhere in sight.

Geo was manning the desk, his eyes focused intently on the screens. Pop thought that the man had to be commended for his dedication. The young man didn't pay any attention to the swarm of forensic techs, patrolling the lobby. There wasn't enough room for all of them in the elevator after all. Most were there just for show.

When the Inspector approached the security guard, and his eyes fell on the screens, his eyebrows shot upward. Only one screen showed the reflection of some corridors, but of course, it wasn't the one the guard's eyes surveyed. The object of the man's attention hosted an action movie, featuring a contemporary Bruce Lee, whose name Pop had never been pressed to find out.

The officer shook his head and then inquired, "Where are the two women who found the body?"

To his dismay, he didn't receive any answer. The action of the movie had gripped Geo in its claws, and the man's pupils couldn't leave the screen.

Pop shook his head and then knocked on the desk. "Anybody home?" he barked, and the young man practically jumped a foot up.

"What...What.... What's the problem here?" Geo managed to mumble after he stuttered for a couple of seconds. His eyebrows bunched on his forehead, and the man belatedly remembered to pause the film.

"The witnesses? Where are they, man?" the officer bad-mugged the security guard.

"There, in the back office," the man pointed to a door on the right of the corridor opening behind him. "Anything else?" he groused, his eyes stealing toward the screen.

THE MAN IN THE ELEVATOR

Pop sighed inwardly. *'If they were watching the screens like that when the crime took place, it's no wonder that a murderer splattered with blood simply vanished,'"* the man reflected with bitterness. Shaking his head in dismay, he started toward the office Geo had shown to him.

When he reached the door, the wailing inside the room made him cringe. The officer practically turned around to leave, but that wasn't possible.

He sighed deeply, gathered his courage and knocked briefly on the door. Then, he stepped inside. The view before his eyes didn't make him happy at all.

CHAPTER FOUR

One pair of eyes turned to the door inquiringly when Alex Pop stepped into the room. For a brief moment, the officer took note of the flicker of curiosity in Ana-Maria's hazel eyes, but he dismissed it without qualms. After all, his presence always brought the same reaction in all witnesses' gaze, and he had become immune over the time.

Then, Pop's eyes swept over the other woman. This one was crying bitterly, holding her head in her shaky hands.

The afternoon sunrays filtered through the blinds and lit the red of the woman's hair. For a fleeting moment there, the man gazed at the enflamed curls mesmerized. But then, he shook his head imperceptibly and closed the door quietly behind him.

"I'm Police Inspector Alex Pop," he introduced himself, turning back toward the two women, and his tone of voice sounded rough even in his ears. The man cleared his voice, slightly embarrassed under the scrutiny of Ana-Maria's wide eyes.

'*Another one who bites the dust,*' the woman reflected ruefully with an inward shrug.

It wasn't as if Ana-Maria hadn't liked Liza. She did, and quite a lot. They wouldn't have been friends otherwise. But then, that didn't stop her from noticing that the woman threw a cone of shadow over any other female present in her proximity. Men were attracted to her in drones.

'*And this one hasn't even seen her eyes or heard her voice yet,*' the young woman continued with her bitter ruminations.

However, at the same time, from under her lashes, she measured the man before her eyes with concealed interest. Up to that moment, she had been lucky enough not to make a detective's acquaintance so his presence stirred her curiosity.

Still, the policeman's appearance was a far cry from what the TV series portrayed. He wasn't a tall man with hard eyes, and a severe mouth. Quite the opposite. The man couldn't have been one inch over 5.7 feet tall, and the young woman just knew that she would be looking straight into his eyes if she had been standing.

'*I knew it. Both movies and books lie. I don't think I've seen a male over six feet tall with broad shoulders and strong thighs,*' the woman smirked, assessing the man. '*The tall ones are usually lanky or rod-thin.*'

His eyes reminded Ana-Maria of the hazelnuts she used to be so fond of in the past, a lifetime away. She would gather as many as she could whenever she would go on a hike through the forests during her childhood years.

The corners of the man's mouth turned upward in a whimsical smile, as if he had known that she measured him critically.

'*This is a man who looks at the world with unconcealed irony,*' Ana-Maria concluded. '*He's probably got a sharp tongue, good to cut one to ribbons if he felt like it.*'

The woman would have liked to read the Police Inspector's thoughts right then. But then, the man had gone back to watching Liza's hair with so much intent that Ana-Maria wondered how her friend hadn't felt his eyes on her yet.

'*Or maybe she has,*' she reflected. After all, she was well-aware of the usual tricks Liza liked to play when she wanted to drive a guy crazy. The woman wasn't a shrinking violet, and her present emotional outburst was out of the ordinary.

Unwilling to continue witnessing the man's bewitchment, Ana-Maria's eyes lowered to the man's mouth again. It fascinated her with its full and soft lips. '*Yep, not bad for kissing,*' she naughtily thought.

Suddenly, she became aware that the man had turned his eyes back on her, and she blushed violently. The woman knew that the officer couldn't have read her mind, but still, she felt conspicuous under his scrutiny.

Pop's eyebrow shot up on his forehead for a few seconds. '*I wonder what is going through her mind when she looks at me,*' he reflected, but then, he shrugged negligently and said, "I understand that the two of you found the body in the elevator."

The next second, the redhead burst into louder sobs, and the man grimaced. Ana-Maria tried to hide her grin, witnessing his discomfort, but she didn't succeed in being fast enough. The man had shifted his eyes toward her again, and his pupils turned darker.

"Yes, we did," Ana-Maria chose to answer to his inquiry. She couldn't turn time back anyway, and she did enjoy his reactions.

Liza bawled louder, and now the woman's narrow and delicate shoulders shuddered vigorously.

Alex breathed deeply to regain his patience, and then, he observed in a quiet tone of voice, "I have serious doubts that I could interview her now. Would it be possible to find someone else to comfort her so that I could talk to you at least?" he asked Ana-Maria aside.

Ana-Maria tilted her head and then nodded. The woman liked how he thought. She would have enjoyed a few moments alone with him far from Liza and her bewitching powers.

Brimming with impatience, the young woman fished her cell phone out of the back pocket of her jeans and browsed through her contacts. She chose one and dialed the number.

It took quite a few seconds for her call to be answered, and by then, Alex had already lost the thin layer of patience he had just gathered. The man started jingling the coins in his pocket and balanced on the balls of his feet.

"Hi there, Maria. I don't know if you have heard what happened," Ana-Maria started to speak fast, albeit very sweetly.

Both eyebrows hiked up Alex's forehead when he heard the woman's tone. He doubted she was as sweet as she wanted to convey. The man had already noticed the shrewdness in her eyes and would have bet without hesitation that the woman didn't have a sweet bone in her entire body.

"Ah, I see that you haven't heard about Dan yet. Anyway, Liza is in a very bad frame of mind right now, and the police need someone to comfort her, you know. And..."

Apparently, her interlocutor interrupted the woman. Ana-Maria stopped speaking and listened impatiently to her colleague. Soon enough, her eyebrows bunched on her forehead, and her eyes thundered.

"No, not me. That was the point of my call. The police wants to talk to me now, and it seems that it is impossible to do so with Liza here," she replied in a huff, unpleasantly surprised by something she was told.

Ana-Maria wasn't mother material in her good days. Besides, she had already had enough of coddling Liza that day. The woman needed some space far from her friend's emotional turmoil.

A small smile tugged at the corners of Alex's mouth when he perceived the change in the woman's voice. *'Now, this is the real one. As I have thought, there's no sweet bone in her entire body,'* he mused, shaking his head imperceptibly. Fascinated, his eyes zeroed in on the angry lights flickering in the woman's pupils.

Suddenly, Ana-Maria noticed his amusement and stood up, turning her back to him. *'I can't keep my calm once, at least once, damn it,'* she admonished herself. The woman had wanted to leave the Inspector with a different impression.

'But how the heck could I keep my calm when my words fall on deaf ears? Why the heck did you think I called, dummy?' she berated her colleague in her mind, not listening to the woman's lengthy discourse.

Maria's words just waltzed by her ears, and Ana-Maria failed to realize that she was doing the very thing of which she had accused her friend.

"All right," she interrupted Maria. "It's pointless to debate what's what now," she continued. "Just ask Alina to send someone here for Liza," she demanded in a tone of voice more appropriate to a general.

'*A wolf in sheep's clothing*,' Alex thought, and his lips twitched. He didn't bother to mask his reaction because Ana-Maria still showed him her back.

"Yes, it would be a good idea to soothe her with some tea or coffee," Ana-Maria approved her colleague's words, but she had to stop again because the other one seemed to be talking some more.

Alex tilted his head on the side and watched the woman with analytical eyes. Her tense back, as well as her fist clenched on the side, showed that she was at the end of her rope.

"Really? Is that what you are all interested in, now?" she shouted, and Alex cringed. "No, you won't get your snacks. Of course," she continued in a biting tone of voice, "you can ask the police to allow you to pick them up off the elevator floor. They're probably seasoned with Dan's blood, but what the heck, you can have a go at them with my wholehearted blessing," the woman concluded sarcastically.

Apparently, Maria expressed her displeasure with the woman's words, but Ana-Maria just shrugged. When people were callous, she could be too.

"Anyway," Ana-Maria cut it to the chase, "ask Alina to send someone here. If not, I will take the time to bring Liza on the floor and leave her with you. You know she can carry on until dawn, if she feels like it," she ended the conversation maliciously and disconnected the call.

Her deep sigh reached Alex's ears, and the man shook his head again. The woman turned to him suddenly, and the policeman schooled his features not to show a thing.

"Don't worry," she waved her hand negligently. "Someone will be here shortly. I don't believe that they would want that on the floor," she tilted her head toward her friend. "How do you feel about some coffee?" she inquired, brusquely striding toward the door with purposeful steps.

Her action surprised Pop, and the policeman stared at her back nonplussed. "I beg your pardon?" he finally managed to say through his teeth. His head started pounding. With one woman crying her eyes out and another playing roles, he had had enough.

"I asked whether you wanted some coffee," Ana-Maria turned her head to him, without breaking her stride. "I need some, and it wouldn't be difficult to bring one for you too," she pointed out, reaching for the door knob.

Alex cleared his throat a couple of times, and then his eyes shifted toward the woman still sitting down and crying her eyes out. He would have liked some coffee, and besides he couldn't forbid Ana-Maria to go and take one. Still, he would have preferred not to be left with a woman who was wailing as if the entire world had ended. Now and then, Liza's sobs reached high notes, and they scratched his ears, sending sharp pains through his skull.

Ana-Maria tried to hide a satisfied grin and waved her hand with nonchalance. "You'll survive," she said with conviction. "Now, do you want coffee or not? And if you do, would it be espresso or cappuccino? Black, with sugar....," she gesticulated. "You know... The works."

Alex looked at her askance, without masking his displeasure. However, he knew that he had to give in. "Espresso, no sugar," he accepted defeat gracefully.

THE MAN IN THE ELEVATOR

"Coming right away," Ana-Maria threw the officer a catlike smile, and a diabolic light played in her pupils. She left the room with a springy step, and Alex shook his head behind her.

'*Should I be afraid that she will try to poison me?*' he wondered.

CHAPTER FIVE

Ana-Maria returned with the coffee cups just a few seconds before someone knocked timidly on the door. Without ceremony, Ana-Maria pushed one of the cups toward Pop, and then she strode to the door with big steps and opened it.

A willowy dark-blonde girl, barely eighteen, in Alex's opinion, smiled at them.

"I came for Liza," she said in near whisper, tilting her head toward the redhead who was still going strong.

'*I wonder when her tears will dry,*' Pop sighed inwardly. The woman had been crying for quite a while now, and the man didn't understand where she found the strength to go on.

"Be my guest," Alex replied in a dry tone of voice. "If she stops crying, maybe you could let me know," he asked the young woman.

The blonde girl nodded in earnest, and the Inspector was afraid that the glasses perched precariously on her nose would fall. The man cringed every time the young woman bobbed her head and prayed that she would stop.

Ana-Maria left her cup on the table and touched Liza's shoulder. "Liza, Carmen came to take you upstairs, girl. I understand that they made some tea for you. Is it all right?"

"No, it's not all right," the woman suddenly jumped off her chair and shouted with more force than anyone would have expected. At the same time, she threw her hands dramatically into the air.

Alex watched her fascinated, and not only because of the show. He noticed that the forest green of her eyes swam in tears, and her eyelids were puffy, but the woman still looked stunning.

Ana-Maria grimaced when she took note of the man's fascination with Liza. She shook her head with dismay. '*I'm afraid this train has left the station, girl*,' she reflected. '*Another guy who's off limits.*'

"Why isn't it all right?" she turned back to more pressing matters and asked her friend in a soothing tone of voice despite of her growing anger.

"Dan is deaaaaad!" she wailed.

'*Tell me something that I don't know*,' Ana-Maria snapped mutely. "We were talking about some tea for you," she tried to steer her friend away from the subject of her ex-boyfriend's death.

"How could I drink tea if he's dead?" Liza huffed and shoved Ana-Maria away with remarkable strength.

'*She might be heartbroken, but she still has some spirit*,' the Inspector thought although he considered the woman's behavior bordering on childish.

"I remember just fine that less than one hour ago you were saying that you didn't care about him anymore," Ana-Maria snapped at Liza, forgetting everything about her good intentions.

THE MAN IN THE ELEVATOR

The woman braced her hands on her hips and stared Liza down ruthlessly. She was sick and tired of her friend's show.

"That was then," Liza shouted. "Now, I care," she stomped her foot on the floor.

"You can continue caring about him upstairs as well," Ana-Maria pointed out, and her mouth became a thin line.

The woman had hoped she would have a chance to impress the Inspector if Liza was out of the picture, but she wasn't so sure about that right now. Not only her friend didn't budge, but unfortunately, the policeman had already seen the not so nice side of herself.

"Or maybe you feel like answering some questions now," Alex intervened.

The man wanted to move his investigation along although the dynamic between the two women interested him.

Nonetheless, Alex regretted his words immediately. Liza shifted her eyes toward him, and she burst into fresh tears after gazing at him inquiringly for a couple of seconds.

'*Here we go again,*' the man sighed inwardly and opened his arms to show that he gave up.

The willowy girl shook her head and approached her two colleagues. She slid her arm around Liza's shoulders and squeezed her gently.

"I know you're distressed right now, sweetie," Carmen whispered to Liza soothingly. "I understand why. I'd be too if I were in your shoes," she admitted. "However, you need to come with me and have some nice hot tea. It will help you, I promise," she continued crooning.

Liza dipped her head with hesitation, but then, she allowed Carmen to lead her to the door, under Ana-Maria's narrowed eyes and the Inspector's baffled expression. The man hadn't expected that the kid would succeed where the other woman had failed.

After Carmen and Liza left the room, the man shifted his gaze toward Ana-Maria and assessed her stance. The woman's breasts were heaving. She was definitely cross.

"Now, we can have our discussion," Pop invited her to sit down, waving his hand toward one of the chairs around the round table.

The woman looked at him sideways. Suddenly, she didn't care that they had been left alone. *'What's the point after all?'* she shrugged visibly, and Alex's eyes slightly widened.

'I think it would be illuminating to have a stroll through this woman's mind,' he mused, taking a seat at the table as well.

The man laid the cup of coffee before him and braced his forearms on the table, intertwining his fingers.

"So, how did you find the body?" he thought of asking first.

Ana-Maria looked at him from under her lashes. *'Are you stupid, or what? The answer is obvious, silly,'* she thought, and the corners of her mouth lifted upward in an ironic grin.

The man was watching her intently, and her reaction made his eyebrow shot up his forehead. *'She's having fun at my expenses,'* he concluded.

The woman shrugged and then said, "We pressed the elevator button to call it and when the doors opened, we noticed the body on the floor," she said in a crisp tone of voice. Still, the implication that anyone would have thought of that remained suspended in the air.

"That I imagined," the man replied dryly. "I was asking what made you take the elevator," he pointed out.

"We usually take the elevator to get to our floor. We work on the seventh floor, you know. I don't really feel like exercising so much," Ana-Maria replied, and her eyes shone mischievously.

The Inspector ground his teeth and re-assessed the woman. She made it difficult on purpose.

"Where had you been that you needed the elevator?" the man groused.

"Just out," she shrugged.

"All right, expand on everything that happened before the elevator doors opened," Alex decided to ask. The woman's attitude strained his patience.

"Everything?" her eyes flickered. "It will take a lot of time. Can you establish a time frame?" she asked, her voice bubbling with laughter.

'*Yep, it is clear. Either she's bored and looking for fun or she has something against the police in general or me in particular,*' the man surmised.

"Let's try a different approach," he proposed. "Where did you go before coming into the building with the intention of taking the elevator?" he asked, and this time, he tried to sound as indifferent as possible.

'*I won't give you the satisfaction of rattling me,*' the man thought, although his knuckles betrayed him. Alex had clinched his fingers so hard that his knuckles had whitened.

The young woman's lips twitched when her eyes swept fleetingly over his hands. She brought her cup to her lips and sipped, watching the man unnervingly over the rim.

"We took a break and went to buy some snacks," Ana-Maria finally revealed, and the lights in her eyes danced.

"Did you meet the victim during your errand?" the policeman inquired.

Ana-Maria shook her head. "No, we didn't. He had left for lunch earlier. I heard him ask a guy on the third floor about the usual time one his female colleagues went out for lunch," she explained.

"What for?" the man asked with puzzlement.

"Not hard to deduce, detective," the woman retorted, stressing the word '*detective*'. '*You're a policeman after all,*' she thought with derision. '*You shouldn't need supplementary explanations. It's not difficult to read between the lines,*' she reflected, looking at the man haughtily.

Ana-Maria had already given up on arousing the detective's interest, so she felt free to talk to him without any artifices. The woman knew from experience that when a guy was hooked up on Liza, she didn't have a chance.

The Inspector chose to drink his coffee in one go. He experienced an unusual impulse—to curl his fingers around the woman's neck and squeeze. Her impertinence bothered him.

"All right, I see. So you haven't seen him while you were out."

Ana-Maria just shook her head, and then, she started drumming her fingers on the top of the table. She enjoyed the man's voice. It sounded thick and soft at the same time. '*Like an old whiskey, I suppose,*' she mused. She also enjoyed the reprieve from work, although work didn't bother her too much. '*But what's the point after all?*' she wondered.

"All right, you went to buy snacks. I noticed your friend seemed much more attached to the victim. Had she said anything about him while you were out? And what happened when she found the body?" Alex asked, his eyes stubbornly fixed on the woman's face, even though the rhythmic movement of her fingers drove him crazy.

"Funny, you know. We were just talking about him," Ana-Maria answered with a faraway expression in her eyes. "Liza was just telling me that Dan had been banned from the fourth club," she mused.

"How come?" Alex asked.

"How come what?" she asked him peevishly and had the surprise to see those soft lips turning hard.

"How come he was banished from the club?" the policeman asked, and his impatience rang in his voice.

"Oh, that," the truth dawned on Ana-Maria. "He jumped on a table and started dancing," she explained.

"I don't imagine people are banished for such a trivial thing," Alex observed dryly.

"They are if they take their clothes off in the process," Ana-Maria countered.

"I see," the man nodded. '*I imagine clubs don't like impromptu striptease,*' he concluded. "So you two were talking about his last adventure in the club when you found him dead on the elevator floor," Alex surmised.

"Yeah, something like that," Ana-Maria approved. '*It took you long enough to get to this conclusion. Poor Dan! He might not get his revenge,*' she thought, not impressed with the policeman's deduction power.

41

Alex read her thought with accuracy and annoyance flashed in his eyes.

"I understand you worked with the victim for some time," he grudgingly continued with his line of questioning.

"Yes, I did. Over three years, as a matter of fact," she approved and drained the rest of her coffee. "So what?" she asked with a shrug.

"So maybe you can tell me what kind of man he was," Alex replied in a hard tone of voice.

Ana-Maria took the time to think over his question, without averting her eyes from the policeman's.

"Dan was... a conundrum, if you want. Hardworking, but superficial at times, caring, but completely insensitive to other people's needs when it suited him... And oh, yes, a ladies' man. The more, the better. Imagine a butterfly wandering from one flower to another without ever stopping for a longer time," she smiled ruefully.

"Were you one of those.... Flowers?" the policeman inquired nosily, and a cynical grin fleeted on his lips. The man was satisfied that he could pay the woman back for all her unflattering thoughts related to him.

Ana-Maria's eyes widened, and for a few moments, the woman just stared at him nonplussed. Then, she burst into joyful laughter and shook her head.

"You missed the target, Inspector," she replied through peals of laughter.

"I don't know what you mean," the man retorted angrily, but a slight blush spread on his cheekbones.

"You know, all right," Ana-Maria countered and shook her head once more. "First of all, until a couple of months before, I was in a relationship, and that for a few years. Second of all, Dan has specific requirements when it comes to his women, you see," she waved her hand. "He prefers busty women and pouty lips," the woman informed him.

When she saw that the man glanced at her not very small bust, she grinned. "Yep, I have that, but I lack in the other department," Ana-Maria said in a dry tone of voice.

Instantly, the man's eyes shifted swiftly at her face. "I didn't mean..."

"Yeah, yeah, I know," she flapped her hand dismissively. The woman didn't mind his wandering eyes.

"Anyway," the man tried to bring the discussion back on track, "was there any other woman in your department who has gone out with Dan?"

"Besides Liza, you mean," Ana-Maria surmised, and the policeman nodded. "Well, probably another three or four," she shrugged.

"Carmen?" Alex inquired.

"Too shy for his type. And besides, her lips are thin," the woman explained.

"Then who else?" the man groused.

"Isabella, I think, but that was about two years ago," the woman replied pensively. "Recently... I don't know... It was Adriana, but she left the department a few months ago... Oh, yes, Alina. She also had a brief fling with him," her eyes sparked with pleasure when she remembered that short relationship.

"Something funny about it?" Alex asked, feeling the woman's concealed amusement.

"In a way," Ana-Maria admitted. "From what I heard, Alina was the first woman in his life who sent him packing. Usually, it was the other way around," she pointed out.

"I see," Alex replied pensively. "Any hard feelings about his usual approach?"

"Not in our department. Liza made a huge scene, and Dan took an absence of leave for a couple of weeks to give her the time to cool off, but otherwise, no. Anyway, women usually knew from the beginning what was what. One of Dan's redeeming qualities was that he always presented his lack of steadiness up front. He always warned women that they couldn't expect more than a couple of weeks or a month at most in his company."

"Interesting, Alex concurred. "Any enemies that you know of?"

Ana-Maria shook her head, but then she reconsidered.

"A couple of months ago, there was a woman. She stalked him a few evenings in a row and threw invectives at him. I know she said she would kill him, but I am sure it was just her broken heart that was talking."

"I can't hope that you knew her and could give me a name," the man tilted his head inquiringly.

"Your assessment is correct," Ana-Maria replied dryly. "I wasn't interested enough to ask. But maybe Liza could enlighten you," she suggested.

"Why do you think she knows?" the detective asked her with curiosity.

"Because that was the woman who stole Dan from her. At least, that's what Liza said. I don't see Liza meekly staying aside and not asking any questions. Dan was wrong about her. Liza likes to cling," she grimaced.

"Besides that woman whose name you don't know, could you name any of Dan's enemies?" Alex asked, watching the woman sideways. He couldn't tell if Ana-Maria's last sentence was a warning for him or just a cold assessment of her friend's character.

"Dan was a wacky one, I'll admit. But people either liked him or steered away from him. I don't remember discussions or quarrels. Of course, if you don't count the squabble he had with Cristian, one of our colleagues," she corrected herself.

"About what was that?" the policeman asked.

Ana-Maria burst into laughter again and shook her head.

"Now what's funny?" Alex frowned.

The woman waved her hand and tried to regain her composure at the same time. She wiped off her eyes with the tips of her fingers and shook her head, a whimsical smile ensconced in the corners of her mouth.

"I apologize. You couldn't know, of course," she finally replied, waving her fingers. "It's absurd to ask about the subject of the quarrel. You see, it could be anything from Dan's passing by Cristian's station to one of Dan's shocking jokes. You never know with Cristian. I can say he quarreled with everybody on the floor. I have heard some rumors that he has managed to alienate people from other floors as well... Cristian is... Let's face it. The man is special," Ana-Maria concluded.

"Yes, he must be in order to alienate so many people," the policeman murmured.

Alex rubbed his forehead with the tips of his fingers. He had the feeling that the entire interview was a waste of time. The man just wanted to excuse himself politely when a knock sounded at the door.

CHAPTER SIX

B oth Ana-Maria and Alex turned to the door as one. The woman's eyebrows got lost under her bangs, and she turned her head toward the policeman.

"Come in," Alex said, and the door opened timidly.

A young man, maybe not even twenty-five, loomed at the door, reluctant to pass over the threshold.

'*Yep, over six feet tall and rod-thin, as I thought,*' Ana-Maria noticed with satisfaction. She always enjoyed being right.

For a moment, the woman had the feeling that the man had dressed entirely in black, but she spotted a splash of white in the opening of his coat. A mop of inky-black hair fell on his left eyebrow, and his light blue eyes shone with hesitation.

'*Hmm, he's not bad looking,*' Ana-Maria admitted, but then she shifted her gaze toward Pop and assessed him again. The eyes of the man shimmered like liquid amber. '*I think I prefer his cognac eyes and rebellious russet hair. Too bad that that boat has already sailed away,*' she reflected, not without sadness.

"The Police Chief-Commissioner sent me to assist you with the investigation, sir," the young man said, and the tip of his ears turned scarlet under Pop's hard eyes.

'He's lying,' Pop concluded. '*The Police Chief-Commissioner sent him to keep an eye on me. Burada has probably already called to let him know that I started the investigation all by myself.*'

"Very well, come in. This is Valentin Bancila," Alex mentioned for Ana-Maria's benefit, without bothering to turn his eyes to her. "He's a fellow Police Inspector," he specified, while Bancila bowed his head toward the woman.

The Inspector wasn't aware, but his eyes had narrowed, while he was looking at his younger colleague steadily. At the same time, his fingers clinched in a tight fist.

Ana-Maria wondered what was going on between the two of them because it was clear that Alex Pop had a bone to pick with the other man. Still, the woman smiled sweetly at the younger Inspector even though the man didn't stir any kind of interest in her.

The young woman wondered how both men shared the rank of Police Inspector although Pop was about ten years older than the newcomer. Pop glanced at her and understood her puzzlement. The gap in age between the two police officers was telling after all.

Actually, both men had studied the law before becoming policemen, but Valentin Bancila joined the law enforcement forces immediately after graduation.

That fact had saddened his family greatly, and they still hadn't forgiven the young man. Everyone in the Bancila family had dreamed of having their very own Take Ionescu in the clan. That was why they considered that Valentin's abdication from his duty, as it had been spelt by their wishes, represented a vicious betrayal.

THE MAN IN THE ELEVATOR

Alex Pop followed a very different path. First, the man joined the military, and as a result, he had the opportunity to witness first-hand the metallic and acrid taste and smell of the war while spending a tour of duty in Afghanistan. When that ended, he joined the Peace Corps. At the time, the man was dreaming of building a better world.

Three years down the road, he was left with the bitter taste of futility. His efforts didn't do anything else but patch up a thing here and there.

Disillusioned, Pop returned into the country and made a cold analysis of the legal arena. After a careful review of a lawyer's life in Bucharest in the twenty-first century, the man shuddered with horror and chose to follow a career in the police force.

Alex Pop began working with Police Chief-Commissioner Baranga just a few months before Bancila came, but his younger colleague started calling him 'sir' and never stopped.

Alex didn't have anything against the young man. Yet, he disliked being put under supervision as if he were a naughty teenager, and that just because he followed his guts in a previous case. After all, he solved that case. It wasn't as if he had failed.

Ana-Maria followed the play of emotions on the faces of both men, and one of her eyebrows rose inquiringly. She would have liked to find out what lay beyond their strange behavior.

Alex noticed her curiosity and schooled his features so that the woman couldn't read too much. Then, he addressed Bancila, "There's another witness. Maybe you will have more luck with her. She's on another floor though. What's her name?" the man turned to Ana-Maria.

"Liza Lazar," the woman replied sweetly, shaking her head imperceptibly. '*This one here has got a mean streak. He's sending that poor lamb to the guillotine,*' she reflected.

Alex guessed her thoughts, and the corners of his mouth turned up. Then, he spoke to his colleague again, "I know that the respective woman is difficult and can cry a river, but who knows, you might have more success with her," he reiterated his previous statement.

"I suppose I'll have to ask the security guards to let me go to that floor," Valentin nodded, although his heart cringed when he heard the bit about a woman crying.

He had a sister. She was just sixteen at the time, but he knew how determined a young woman could be if she wanted to bawl like a banshee.

"You suppose well," Pop agreed with him. "I don't expect you will encounter any resistance from them. Ana-Maria will also accompany you upstairs. We're finished here," he turned to the young woman, whose mien changed.

A shadow crossed the woman's face, and she bit her lower lip. Ana-Maria felt like giving Alex a sharp reply. '*You, wretch!*' she reflected. '*To dismiss me like yesterday's news,*' her eyes thundered.

Alex merely smiled sweetly at her. '*You drove me a merry chase, sweetheart, but I had the last laugh in the end,*' he thought.

"On your way out, please, send the security guard named Georgescu in here," the man turned back to his colleague. "It's time I asked those guards some specific questions," he said in a hard tone of voice.

CHAPTER SEVEN

Georgescu stopped before the open door and knocked on the jamb when he noticed that the Inspector was lost in his thoughts. Alex looked up and with a weak smile invited the man to come inside and close the door behind him. Then, he waved his hand, showing toward the chair across from him.

The old man seemed reluctant at first, but then, he pushed the door shut and strode over to the table. His gait betrayed anything but rush.

Alex could understand the man's reluctance because most people he interviewed displayed the same hesitation when it came to speaking to someone from the police.

The security guard sat down, his eyes carefully analyzing the young man before him. He didn't seem to find what he was looking for and averted his eyes, leaning forward and bracing his arms on top of the table.

"How long have you been working here?" Alex started his questions.

The man arched an eyebrow inquiringly. He didn't understand the purpose of that line of questioning. Still, he answered, "About five years, I think," the man shrugged.

"And before that?" Alex asked.

"Here and there," Georgescu answered. "Buildings change hands more often than you'd think," he explained his nomad career to the policeman.

"I see," Alex replied pensively. "Is it a good job? Here, I mean," he specified.

"It helps me make a living," the man shrugged again. "I can't complain though," he added.

"Did you see anything on the screens when the crime took place?" Alex attacked in force, and his frontal offensive rendered his interlocutor speechless.

The old man gazed at the Inspector askance for a few moments and fidgeted in his chair.

"Any problem with answering the question?" the policeman asked in a hard tone of voice.

The security guard shook his head and ran his shaky fingers through his hair. That was one of the questions he had hoped not to hear.

Then, he started speaking with a brief hesitation, "I can't say I saw anything. I wasn't quite in front of the screen when the murder happened. The man must have been murdered just a little before the women found the body because those elevators are used almost all the time at that hour... The problem is that I went outside to smoke a cigarette... probably about fifteen minutes before, you see. I had just come back into the building when the screams started. I had time only to jump over the turnstile and rush toward the women," Georgescu explained at length with an economy of gestures.

"I see," Alex said with a trace of disappointment in his voice. "Who was manning the station at that time?"

"I left Geo in charge," the old man replied.

"The one who's watching movies instead of surveying the cameras?" the Inspector asked in a sarcastic tone of voice.

The security guard blushed slightly, but then, he nodded. He couldn't have countered that affirmation. It was true after all.

'*I kept telling the pup to pay attention to the screens, damn it all,*' he swore mutely. '*Of course, they are younger and smarter. Now, look what happened,*' he shook his head. '*Look at what mess we have landed in,*' he sighed inwardly.

Alex followed the play of emotions on the man's face and guessed with accuracy the thoughts that passed through his mind.

"Maybe I should talk to this Geo. He might have seen something, even if he was watching a movie," Alex said.

The old man bit his lower lip and then said, "He wouldn't have seen anything. The images from cameras on the first, second, third and fourth floor are on the screen where he played the movie," the man reckoned. When the enormity of the fact hit him, Georgescu paled. "Now what?" he asked in a small voice.

"What do you mean?" Alex inquired with some puzzlement.

"What happens now that he wasn't watching what he should have?" the man asked in a rough tone of voice. His throat felt constricted.

"Well, that is up to your superiors. Of course, there might be a recording...," Alex advanced the idea, but the old man shook his head.

"There's no recording. I have checked," the man admitted. "I knew that you would ask for that. There should have been though. I couldn't check the camera there because I didn't have the time, but something seems to have malfunctioned," Georgescu explained in a tone of voice that conveyed his dismay.

"That's interesting, I would say," Alex murmured, and the security guard nodded his assessment.

"It is," the man concurred. "No camera has malfunctioned until now. And the coincidence is jarring," he pointed out.

"I would like that you don't touch that camera for the time being. I need one of our techs to take a look at it. Is that all right with you?" Alex inquired.

'*As if I had a say in the matter,*' the old man sneered to himself. '*We're already in deep shit. I might even lose my job over this fiasco,*' he thought bitterly.

"No, it isn't a problem. You can have a go at it," Georgescu said afterward.

Alex bowed his head as if he thanked the old man and took his phone out of his pocket. He dialed the headquarters and requested an expert in surveillance devices.

"Tell him to ask for Mr. Georgescu at the front desk. He's the security guard here and will show the technician where to look," he said after he explained the situation. "Good, I will still be here, of course. Mr. Georgescu will tell him where. Thank you," the Inspector concluded his conversation and disconnected the call.

Then, the man looked at the security guard and said, "Someone from headquarters will come in probably half an hour. I hope you're still here to help him with the location and everything," he gazed at the older man meaningfully.

Georgescu nodded wordlessly. '*As if you cared about my opinion,*' the old man thought. '*It's not like I could tell you that my shift ended five minutes ago. I'm already in trouble as it is,*' he reflected and stood up, shaking his head once more. That day didn't progress very well.

"I suppose you're finished with me for the moment," Georgescu said to the Inspector.

"Not quite yet," Alex smiled coldly at the man, and the security guard dropped back in his chair. The Inspector hardly held a grin at bay when he noticed the disappointment on the man's face.

"What else is there?" the man asked, somewhat peevishly.

"I need to know what security measures are in place to reach the upper floors. I also want to know if there is another way to leave the building."

"Well, people can get into the secured area only if they have badges. They need them at the turnstile. Now, someone could leave the building using the mezzanine elevator. They can get off the elevator at mezzanine and leave through the back entrance. They can also use any elevator to go down to the underground parking lot. There are two underground levels," the man explained with a frown on his face.

"Are there cameras on those levels?" Alex leaned forward and intertwined his fingers on the top of the table.

"Yes, there are," the security guard nodded.

"Monitored?" the Inspector asked with slight irony.

The man nodded again. "Yes, the images from those cameras are on the other screen, not the one with the movie," he informed the Police Inspector.

"Then I should talk to Geo and ask him about that," Alex concluded.

"You can try," Georgescu mumbled, but the Inspector still heard him, and a grin tugged at the corners of his mouth.

Alex doubted that Geo had paid any attention to the other screen, but he still had to try and ask the man. "Could you ask him to come here?" he asked the security guard.

"I'll go and call him," the man said in a normal tone of voice, and then rushed toward the door, willing to leave the room faster so that the Inspector couldn't ask him any more questions.

Alex shook his head, his eyes following the man's fast retreat. The Inspector's face betrayed the man's puzzlement. He couldn't believe the incompetence of that security team.

Then, he leaned back in his chair. '*At least they have comfortable chairs around,*' he mused. '*Better than the ones in my office,*' he admitted, not with a little envy.

After a few minutes of waiting, he frowned. '*Where the heck is that Geo?*'

CHAPTER EIGHT

A s the time passed on, and no one came into the room, Alex stood up and started pacing around. It seemed quite dubious that Geo hadn't arrived yet. There were about ten, let's say fifteen paces, from the front desk to the room where the policeman was waiting.

The man waited five minutes more, but his patience was already frayed. He started with heavy steps toward the door and ran into Georgescu, who was about to get into the office.

"Sorry, old man," Alex said automatically. "I haven't seen you there. Where the heck is that Geo? I've been waiting for him forever," the man said in a reproachful tone of voice.

"I don't know, sir," the old man replied in a pathetic voice. "I couldn't find him although I looked for him everywhere. He finished his shift. That is true. But he shouldn't have left like that," the old man said. "He usually has to check with me. And especially today…," the security guard shook his head with disbelief.

Now, Alex noticed the grayness of the man's face with worry. The older man's lips had become a thin line, and he seemed to have difficulty breathing.

"Listen, are you all right?" the policeman inquired, apprehensive that the man would kneel over. The old man didn't seem very steady on his legs either.

"I don't really know, sir," the man murmured, and in the next second, he collapsed.

The Inspector tried to catch the guard, but the man's fall surprised him, and he wasn't fast enough. Georgescu dropped to the floor like a log and a loud thump ensued.

Alex stared at the man crumpled in a heap at his feet with disbelief for a few seconds and then hunched next to him. He checked for pulse and sighed with relief when he found it. The man's pulse was very weak, but still beating.

The detective slapped the man's face a couple of times, but he didn't get any response as reward for his efforts. That made him take his phone out of his pocket and call for an ambulance.

Pop didn't have to wait for a long time. Someone answered his call almost immediately. The policeman insisted on the degree of emergency and demanded that a car be sent there with maximum haste.

When he finished with the call, Alex checked Georgescu's pulse again, afraid that the old man might have died on him already. He breathed deeply with relief when he felt the weak but steady pulse under the tips of his fingers. After a second, Alex decided that he should help the man lie in a better position and stretched his legs.

Then, the Inspector rubbed his temples, his eyes always fixated on the man on the floor. After a brief reflection, he called Police Chief-Commissioner Baranga.

THE MAN IN THE ELEVATOR

"Hello, sir," the policeman greeted his superior. "No, I'm afraid that things aren't going very well," he replied to something Baranga asked him. "I already have a missing witness and another one has just collapsed before my eyes. Police Inspector Bancila is interrogating a witness on a floor upstairs, and I am stuck here with a man who might have had a heart attack for all that I know. Could you send at least one of the Police Sub-Inspector s here, sir?"

Apparently, the Chief-Commissioner started talking because Alex stopped and listened carefully. A tentative smile perched on his lips.

"Yes, indeed, sir. I have never asked for reinforcements. Well, I suppose there is a beginning for everything," he shrugged with indifference.

Alex wasn't keen on asking for help. Yet, he knew better than to jeopardize an investigation because of misplaced pride. That was the moment to prove it. It wasn't as if he had been forced to ask for directions.

CHAPTER NINE

B y the time Police Sub-Inspector Popa joined him, Alex had passed beyond the limit of his patience, and as a rule he was a patient man. The emergency services had already gotten there and just removed Georgescu from the premises.

To Pop's dismay, the paramedics told him that indeed the old man had had a heart attack. However, they estimated that the security guard had chances to fully recover.

That piece of good news took a burden off the policeman's chest. The Inspector wouldn't have liked to bear the responsibility of the old man's demise.

After all, Georgescu's only fault had been not to manage his people closely. The man had been too indulgent. But then, it was true enough that the old man's behavior could be translated into carelessness, as well.

Pop's eyes turned to the dark-skinned Sub-Inspector, who had just stepped into the room. A smile perched on Alex Pop's lips. The Sub-Inspector's appearance always looked just a bit out of the ordinary.

Popa's height came only to the Inspector's shoulder, and his thin silhouette often got lost in dark corridors. With his coloring, people could hardly notice his presence if the space wasn't bright enough.

Still, in spite of his puny appearance, the man did have quite a few commendations under his belt, and Pop always enjoyed working with him. The man's waggish nature brought some color to the darkest investigation.

"Just got here, sir," he greeted Pop. "There's a lady there at the front desk, and she told me that I would find you in here," the man pointed his thumb back toward the corridor.

"That's good," Pop approved. "I haven't seen a woman there before, but probably they had to find someone to hold the front considering the missing guards."

"What's the order, sir?" Popa asked, arching his eyebrows with curiosity.

The man always appreciated Pop. The Inspector never had boring tasks for him and wasn't set in his ways.

"I need you to locate a missing security guard. I only know that his first name is Geo and last name Popescu, I think, but I suppose the lady from the front desk could offer you some more information about the guy," Pop suggested, waving his fingers in the general direction of the door.

"And once I found him?" Popa inquired, arching one of his eyebrows quizzically. The man preferred to have the orders clearly spelled out to him.

"Take him to the headquarters and call me," the Inspector ordered. "Of course, if in the course of your actions you can also determine who his relations are, and what the man is up to, please, feel free to do it. I know you can unbury any secret," Alex said with confidence.

"Consider it done, sir. I'll find him. There's no place he could hide from me," the Sub-Inspector replied in a confident tone of voice, tapping his big nose with a finger.

Pop grinned. People's gossip had reached him even though he didn't show any outward interest in the office prattle. The Inspector had found out that everyone considered that Popa was able to pick up the trace of a person better than a hound.

"Impress me," Pop murmured.

Still, the Sub-Inspector's ears didn't fail the man, and he caught the Pop's words. Popa replied with a wide smile on his angular face, "Don't I always, sir?"

Popa's hooded black eyes lit with amusement for a couple of seconds. Then, he turned around and left the room without another word for Pop, as he was prone to do once he got his orders.

Pop remained alone and looked around for a few seconds. "I think that I'm done here," he said in a loud voice, and then strode purposefully to the door.

'Let's find someone to show me to where Bancila is,' he reflected. 'The poor guy must be sick of all that wailing already,' Alex Pop mused. He remembered just fine the way Liza liked to carry on.

When he got to the front desk, Pop noticed that Popa was still there. He was charming his way into the front-desk attendant's heart, using flattery and flirting without mercy.

Pop waited patiently aside until Popa wrung all possible information from the woman who sat behind the desk. The desk-attendant listened to the dark-haired man, smiling widely and fluttering her lashes.

While eavesdropping on the two people's conversation, a smile would fleet on the Inspector's lips now and then. '*He's a rogue, this Popa,*' he thought. The woman was putty in the Sub-Inspector's hands.

Besides the answers to his questions, Popa also got a piece of paper neatly folded. Pop didn't doubt that the woman, whose name tag dabbed her as Camelia, had written down her phone number for the Sub-Inspector. The woman preferred to give it to him like that only because she had noticed the Inspector's presence.

Camelia's intentions toward Popa were clear enough. Pop had also noticed that a frown would mar the woman's features whenever she shifted her eyes from the Sub-Inspector and glanced at him.

'*I'm a hindrance apparently,*' the Inspector mused and shook his head imperceptibly. '*Still, you'll have to talk to me too, sweetheart,*' he reflected with irony.

At the same time, Alex Pop measured the woman critically. She was already passed over thirty, given her skin's appearance. However, the man had to admit that she still looked good and congratulated Popa mutely for his newest conquest.

Once Popa left, with a last wink for the woman who blushed prettily, Pop breathed with relief. The man had never enjoyed witnessing any kind of flirting rituals. Three were too many when it came to that.

THE MAN IN THE ELEVATOR

Camelia finally turned to him. But then, her smile disappeared as if someone had swiftly wiped it off with a sponge. Her cold blue eyes assessed the man in a couple of seconds and found him lacking.

"So, how can I help you, sir?" the woman asked with indifference. Camelia imagined that the man before her eyes must have been the Police Inspector about whom everybody in the building talked.

'*What for, God knows. He doesn't look like much. Now, the other guy, the swarthy one, that one is something else, indeed,*' the woman mused.

The Inspector arched his right eyebrow questioningly. Pop had a certain idea about the direction of the woman's thoughts, but he doubted that he would like to know them in detail.

"I need to join my other colleague who is interviewing another witness on the seventh floor," the man said matter-of-factly, sparing the woman of any chit-chat.

The woman sighed deeply as if the man had asked her to show him the way to the top of Mount Everest. Then, she dialed a number, frowning at Pop all the while.

CHAPTER TEN

Because of the glass walls of the room, Pop had the possibility to see Bancila and the object of the Inspector's interview even before walking into the conference room.

Alex observed how Bancila leaned toward Liza, asking her something. Of course, the woman was still crying.

'*I wonder if there is anything else she can do,*' he reflected with malice.

Moreover, the man noticed that her sobs seemed to become louder every time the Inspector opened his mouth. That prompted him to roll his eyes in disbelief.

On Liza's other side, Carmen whispered soothing words to her colleague and patted her arm reassuringly. However, the tense line of the young woman's shoulders proved that this one had also had enough of that spectacle and was getting ready to move on.

'*I doubt anyone could take it for a longer time, regardless of their best intentions,*' Pop thought.

The man sighed deeply at the sight of the group but resolved to go inside. He drew his shoulders back and pushed the door open. Three heads turned to him with different expressions.

Valentin seemed relieved to see that reinforcements arrived. The man had entertained the thought of banging his head on the table before him for the last half an hour. The interview wasn't going well, and he had gathered no pertinent information so far.

The willowy girl glanced at Alex quizzically at first, and then the corners of her mouth turned up shyly. Soon enough, her entire face flourished under a wide smile, which changed her completely. The serious meekly mien disappeared, and her eyes sparked with a warm light, which took Alex by surprise and made him look at her more attentively.

'*She's too damn young and innocent, though, man,*' he reflected, and the image of the other woman he had met that day popped into his mind. '*Yep, that's more up my alley,*' Alex reckoned. '*Not easy to break, I suppose,*' the man concluded.

The elusive Liza, whose eyes always shimmered in a well of tears, glanced at him askance. After a brief assessment of the man before her eyes, the woman didn't believe that she could play the same game as she had done with his fellow until then.

"How's it going?" Alex inquired, tilting his head with curiosity.

'*He looks like a confused dog,*' Carmen thought, and her eyes stole a glance toward Valentin. '*The older one might be stronger and wiser, but this one is just what a man should be,*' she concluded with an unusual determination for a woman of her age.

"Not very well, sir," Valentin admitted with a deep sigh. "It's like pulling teeth," he explained, opening his arms with resignation.

"I see," Alex Pop said and took a seat next to his colleague. "What seems to be the problem here?" he asked with a pointed look toward the woman with a mourning face.

"I'm not in a good frame of mind to answer to your questions right now, and you should have known that. You should have shown some more consideration for my state," the woman replied with obvious reproach in her weepy voice. "I've just lost a very dear man, and I can't be rushed into anything. I need the time to mourn," she tapped her finger onto the top of the table decisively, her actions in obvious contrast with the picture she was drawing about herself. "I need to be allowed to grieve," she said, forgetting about her delicate condition for a few moments.

"I don't doubt that you need a period of mourning, miss," Alex nodded with understanding. "I understand the need to grieve when you lose someone dear, especially in such horrible circumstances," he acknowledged her feelings.

Nonetheless, the man couldn't stop noticing that the woman was capable to express her wishes strongly, in spite of her distress.

"However, I find it strange that you don't also feel that you need us to find the murderer," the Police Inspector continued in a hard voice. "Especially in such circumstances, people do ask for revenge, and quite vocally, even if they don't necessarily believe in the motto that justice must prevail above everything," he pointed out meaningfully.

Liza blushed violently, the color of her face competing with her red-rimmed eyes. The young woman kept silent for a couple of seconds, at a loss of words, but then, she frowned.

"I don't like what you're implying," she snapped at the Inspector angrily, and her eyes thundered.

Alex merely shrugged. '*If the shoe fits...,*' he mused, but his eyes never left the woman's face.

"I'm not implying anything," the man waved his hand negligently. "Still, I can't stop wondering why you're so reluctant to answer a few questions," he pointed out. "Your answers might help to put a killer behind bars," he stressed out.

"I'm not," Liza huffed. "Shoot away," she waved her fingers anxiously toward the Inspector.

"Were you having a relationship with the deceased?" Alex asked, folding his hands on the top of the table. He looked straight at Liza, but he didn't fail to notice the ironic grin hidden in the corners of Carmen's mouth.

"I... We were in a relationship," Liza stuttered, and her fingers twitched on the table.

"Now, at the time of his demise?" Alex's left eyebrow arched upward, proving that the man didn't believe the woman's statement. Ana-Maria didn't have any reason to lie to him after all.

Liza blushed again and fidgeted in her chair. She averted her eyes for a few seconds, but then the woman dared to look back at him.

"No, not now. Our relationship ended a couple of months ago," she admitted.

"Any special reason for that?" the man asked softly. He didn't feel like inflicting any kind of pain on someone just for the sake of having fun.

Liza shrugged, and her eyes fixated on her hands. From the corner of his eye, Alex noticed the twitch of Carmen's lips. '*She knows something,*' he thought.

"So, how did things go between you and Dan? That was his name, if I remember correctly," Alex asked. "After the break up between the two of you, I mean," the man thought to specify.

Another annoying shrug stole his eyes. '*This Liza definitely likes to mask everything under those shrugs and infernal sobs,*' the man concluded. '*She's a master at deflecting questions.*'

"Not much of a difference," the woman said, and Carmen's eyes widened.

'*Surely, we have to talk to this girl,*' Alex decided. '*She seems to be a fountain of information.*'

"Do you have any idea what Dan did during the last few days, and if he angered anybody so much that that person needed to take his life?" the man inquired.

As Alex Pop expected, the woman shrugged once more. He sighed inwardly, fed up with the woman's theatrical behavior.

"I know that he went to clubs and got banned from another club recently," Liza replied in an indifferent tone of voice. "I've also heard that he broke up with his last girlfriend a couple of weeks before and showed interest in a new girl.... I don't think he did anything else...," she finished her discourse, brushing her restless fingers through the flame of her hair.

"I see," Alex nodded. "I think you should take the day off and go home, miss. It would help with your... mourning and frame of mind. If you don't mind, though, please, leave your coordinates with my colleague here," the man tilted his head toward the younger Inspector. "If we still need to contact you, we'd like to be able to do it," Alex stated in a hard tone of voice so that the woman understood that he didn't intend to take *no* for an answer.

Liza nodded hesitantly, and shifted her eyes toward the younger Inspector. Valentin took out his phone and opened the note-taking application. Then, he looked up at the woman and waited for her to dictate her phone number and address to him.

Meanwhile, Pop turned to Carmen, who was getting ready to leave the room.

"I'd like to have a word with you afterward if you don't mind," he said aside to the young woman, and Carmen nodded, sitting back in her chair, although with some reluctance.

Liza threw a black look in the younger woman's direction. Her eyes narrowed to slits, as if she wanted to warn Carmen to watch her mouth.

Carmen fidgeted under the intensity of the redhead's eyes and preferred to look at the top of the table. A shaky finger pushed her glasses up on her nose, and then brushed a wayward lock of hair behind her ear.

Valentin helped Liza to the door and shut the door behind her. A moment later, he sighed deeply with evident relief and shook his head.

Only afterward, the man turned around and said, "That woman... She's something else, indeed. She could suck up the energy right from your body," he shook his head ruefully once more.

Carmen offered him a wide smile, and the man perked. Alex watched the play between the two young people's actions with interest.

THE MAN IN THE ELEVATOR

'*This is... just thrilling, I'd say,*' the policeman admitted to himself.

Then, the man turned toward Carmen and said, "I'm quite sure you could give us some of the answers we're looking for."

Carmen's eyelids fluttered, hiding her amber eyes for a few moments. Valentin leaned forward, watching the light dance on the woman's skin.

CHAPTER ELEVEN

C armen raised her eyelids, and her undecipherable look hit Valentin in the gut. Alex didn't prove himself immune to the power of the woman's eyes either.

'Just a few more years, and she'll be a reputable force. A guy will not know if he's coming or going,' the man reflected. *'Thank God, I won't be around her at that time.'*

"Yes, I will probably be able to answer some of your questions," the young woman nodded sagely but didn't continue.

Carmen just waited quietly, gazing from one man to the other with her amber shimmering eyes. She folded her hands in her lap, giving the impression of being a timid schoolgirl.

'So far from the truth,' Alex reflected, interpreting correctly the woman's so-called meek appearance. *'I'm afraid she's more dangerous than the weeping willow,'* he thought of Liza.

Valentin cleared his throat and then shifted his eyes toward Alex. He wanted to see if his colleague wanted to start the questioning. Alex merely waved his hand, inviting him to lead the interview.

"I suppose you knew the victim well," Valentin asked Carmen in a quiet tone of voice.

"Yes, as a colleague, I did know him well enough," she approved with a slight nod of her head. "I rarely had the occasion to go out in a group with him, though, so I can't really say that I knew him well as a man," the young woman pointed out.

"But at least you know something about him from what you've seen or heard. Gossip must have reached you. I can't believe that people didn't talk about him," Valentin insisted with frustration.

'*A guy who gets banned from a club for doing a striptease number on a table is a man everybody talks about,*' he reflected.

"If you want hearsay, yes, there has been enough of that," Carmen shrugged, and her eyes shimmered with puzzlement. "I would have thought that you'd prefer to hear some real facts though," she added in a crisp tone of voice, shifting her eyes from a man to another.

Valentin blushed slightly and bit his lips. Alex grinned and shook his head. '*Not so shy now, the little mouse,*' he thought with amusement.

Still, he decided to intervene because his younger colleague seemed to have lost his voice somehow. The man's tongue was in knots.

"That's true," the older Inspector admitted. "We would regularly prefer to hear facts not gossip, but sometimes, we also find some leads to follow from gossip alone. You know the saying '*No smoke without fire*,'" Alex pointed out, waving his fingers meaningfully.

Carmen shrugged negligently and waved her hand toward the two men, "All right, I get it now," she said. "There is not much to say about him, though. I mean from the gossip. A

76

ladies' man, Dan loved to change his girl-friends every few weeks. Some clung to him, but only a few. Apparently, the man knew how to choose them. He struck out only twice, from what I know."

"Probably once with Liza," Valentin chimed in for the first time.

"Yes, indeed," Carmen nodded. "I think Dan's streak of bad luck started with her," Carmen said pensively, a far-away look in her gaze. "The girl that Dan dated after Liza turned out being as clingy as Liza was. Then, he got banned out of four clubs, one after another," the young woman shook her head. "And now the final blow," she observed in a morose tone of voice.

"Do you happen to know the name of his last girl-friend?" Valentin inquired leaning forward toward the woman, and not only because he wanted to hear her soft voice better.

"I think it was Alice or something of the kind. I saw her only once when she came and made a big scene right here downstairs. The security team had to remove her from the premises."

"Did she threaten Dan?" Axel inquired.

"Well," Carmen tilted her head, "I think so," she said, but her tone of voice rang unsure. "She said a lot of things. She swore at him and even attacked him physically. A couple of days afterward, I heard that she keyed his car....," she shook her head once more. "Dan was very proud of that car. He had saved a lot to buy it, after all. I think that the car should still be in the underground parking lot now," the woman informed them.

"Interesting that no one else had mentioned that car to us," Alex murmured, and Valentin just shrugged.

"We should be able to find the license plate of the car, sir," the young Inspector mentioned. "There must be an office somewhere where someone would know which one his parking lot is, I think," he added.

"Yes, there is," Carmen nodded. "You just have to speak to the reception desk on the second floor. They take care of those parking spots. I hear it is quite difficult to get one, but Dan... Let's say that he had some special skills. One of them was persuasion. He could convince almost anyone of anything, especially if that someone was a female," the young woman said, and the corners of her mouth curved upward.

"I think that I will go and check with her, sir," Valentin proposed, although with little enthusiasm, and his eyes ran swiftly toward Carmen.

It was obvious that the young man would have preferred to continue talking with her.

'*Young hearts and spring,*' Alex thought, not without a little sarcasm.

However, the man didn't have any intention to get into his younger colleague's path and stopped Valentin to stand up by putting his hand on his colleague's arm.

"Or I could go there now, and you can continue your interview with Carmen. I suppose that I will be back in about ten minutes or so," the man said, standing up.

He strode over to the door, and both young people who remained in their chairs around the conference table stared at his back nonplussed.

Valentin shook his head when he saw that Alex left the room, indeed, and then turned toward Carmen.

"So this guy, Dan, was interested only in women and cars, from what I can gather," he concluded.

"At first sight, he was," Carmen agreed with reluctance.

"At first sight?" Valentin asked with puzzlement.

"That's what people saw anyway, and very few looked beyond that in order to really see the man," Carmen replied in a hard tone of voice, which prompted Valentin's eyebrows to shot up on his forehead.

The woman hadn't seem very decisive in her opinions until then, and her attitude disconcerted him.

CHAPTER TWELVE

A lex returned to the room just in time to see Valentin show Carmen to the door. The young man's eyes shone with joy, and the young woman seemed a bit flustered.

Alex arched an eyebrow quizzically, and in that very moment, the two young people noticed him, and both blushed violently. Carmen even lowered her gaze, appearing suddenly unsure of herself.

'*I wonder what happened in my absence,*' the older Inspector thought, but the man knew that he couldn't ask his colleague directly. '*Well, maybe the man is in the mood to share,*' Alex shrugged inwardly and then greeted Carmen, who strode with fast steps out of the room.

"I found Dan's car and asked the forensic experts to have a look at it. You can imagine that they didn't like it when I told them that they had to come back for that," Alex explained to Valentin with a grin. "They mumbled a lot."

Alex Pop wasn't above a little malice when the mood struck, and he needed something to lighten up his day after all. He had spent an entire morning in court, rubbing elbows with all sorts of boring individuals, and afterward he started on this case, which didn't seem to be very easy.

The Police Inspector couldn't say that they hadn't gathered some information about the victim although he doubted that they had got the entire picture about Dan. No one could have been as linear as Dan appeared from his colleagues' accounts. People, regardless of their background and their avenues in life, always proved more complex than what they had found out about Dan by then.

Valentin grinned as well. He knew his colleague well enough even if Alex Pop could make him feel quite insecure and uncomfortable sometimes. All in all, Valentin appreciated Alex, and he even was grateful for the man's quiet help and guidance.

Alex might not have been a man of many words, but he knew how to lead someone wordlessly on the right way. Not just a few times, Alex had saved Valentin's green hide in front of their Police Chief-Commissioner.

Baranga didn't fit into the niche of people given to forgiveness. Making a grave mistake and letting that mistake reach the Police Chief-Commissioner's ears without having a solution to fix it could land one into serious trouble. Alex's last sting came to mind while reflecting upon such unforgivable errors.

"Anyway," Alex's voice shook Valentin off his meditation, "what did Carmen tell you about our man?"

Valentin looked up at his older colleague and said, "Apparently, there was more to that man than meets the eye. She said that the guy didn't only have a cavalier and reckless behavior. In a way, it was as if he had led a double life. However, he kept that other life quite hidden. Carmen chanced to notice a different side of him because she happened to be at the right place at the right time."

"Meaning?" Alex lifted his right brow on his forehead and waved his hand impatiently to make the young Inspector continue without convoluted phrases. Another thing Alex abhorred was rambling.

Valentin licked his lips with anxiety. He felt awkward and was afraid that Alex would consider him sappy for talking about such things. However, he answered his colleague's question.

"Apparently, Dan volunteered a lot. He visited an old people's house once a week where he offered food and some of his time. The man gossiped with a few of the old people, played cards with others and even organized a soiree for them once. He paid for absolutely everything. Carmen ran into him there by chance when she went to pay a visit to an old uncle of hers. Dan seemed uncomfortable to be seen there and asked her to keep that chance encounter under the wraps. She spoke to her uncle afterward, and the man told her that Dan was a permanent fixture there. He brought them a lot of joy with his outlandish ideas for brightening their days and his bad jokes. Besides, he had charmed every woman in that retirement house, both staff and pensioners," Valentin shook his head with amusement.

"Interesting individual, indeed," Alex agreed with the conclusion he could read in his colleague's eyes.

"Besides his volunteering there, Carmen said that the man was also involved in rescuing dogs. She went out to smoke a cigarette one evening. The girl doesn't like to smoke where everybody goes and prefers to hide around the building for a bit of peace and quiet. She stumbled upon Dan, who was talking with a guy on the phone about finding homes for a few puppies. From what she overheard, someone had abandoned the dogs on the shoulder of the road, and Dan's connection found them the night before."

"I see," Alex murmured. "I had a feeling that the guy wasn't the sum of the actions and behavior everyone witnessed regularly. So, what else did Carmen tell you?" he shifted his eyes back to Valentin.

"In relation to the case?" Valentin stuttered, and his eyes widened.

He couldn't believe that Alex would ask personal questions. Until then, the man hadn't seemed interested enough to have anything else to do with him but a work relationship, which didn't involve any kind of confessions.

"Do you think I am interested in finding out that you wrung out a date with Carmen?" Alex arched his brow haughtily, looking at the young Police Inspector with unconcealed irony.

"No, of course not, sir," the young man rushed to agree with him.

Alex sighed deeply. "I would really appreciate it if you stopped calling me sir," the man said. "We have the same rank, and my seniority in the force relies only in my working here about six or seven months more than you. And don't tell me about my age," Alex hurried to say, putting up his hand to stop Valentin to utter any kind of nonsense. "I don't feel like spending time reflecting upon my '*advanced*' age," he warned Valentin with a glower.

Valentin swallowed hard. He never knew how to react around Alex.

"All right," the young man said in the end. "Carmen also said that Dan liked to make some bad jokes, and not everyone liked them. There had been a few sparks here and there along the time, of course. Some of the people left the company long time ago and don't seem to have had any other encounter with Dan. Still, during the last three weeks, the man managed to make four people fairly angry, and he came to blows with two of them," Valentin informed him, throwing a glance toward his notes.

"Now you're talking," Alex congratulated the Inspector with a thump on his shoulder. "We do need to talk with those too. First, we'll talk with that Alina who dared to give him his leave papers, so to speak, and then we'll move on to the others. We'll mix the four who interest us with others, so that no one could suspect that we would be interested in them. Everybody will be able to guess that Carmen gave us some info, and I don't see the point to put the girl in the crosshairs with the others," Alex added.

Valentin agreed fully with him, nodding vigorously, which brought another caustic grin on Alex's lips.

"How do we call people in for an interview?" Alex inquired. "Should we just open the door and holler, hoping that someone will come?" he tilted his head toward the open floor that stretched beyond the glass walls of the conference room.

There, rows of desks sat neatly arranged under the strong light of the lamps mounted onto the ceiling.

Valentin laughed and shook his head. '*I'd love to see how that would go,*' he thought. However, he had a strong sense of ridicule and would have liked to be far, far away, the moment Alex would have done that.

"Carmen told me that it would be enough to open the door and ask the girl at that table there to call someone," the young man replied after he stifled his laughter. He pointed toward a girl with curly red hair.

Alex's heart skipped a beat when his eyes fell on the enflamed curls. For a moment there, the man feared that he would have to speak to that unstoppable well of tears named Liza once more.

CHAPTER THIRTEEN

Alina entered the conference room with the confident step of a woman who was deeply aware of her own worth. Her midnight hair cascaded on her shoulders in soft curls, reaching the top of her hips. Both men gazed at her for quite a few seconds, and admiration shimmered in their eyes.

'*Not quite a corporate appearance, I'd say,*' Alex Pop thought.

The woman advanced with supple steps toward the desk, and the men stood up at attention at once. Alex couldn't stop his eyes from wandering along the length of the woman's legs.

'*This woman definitely took ballet classes. Only a ballerina would move with such a wild grace,*' Alex reflected, and unconsciously licked his lips.

Valentin's eyes widened, and the man wiped his hands on his trousers. His palms started sweating the moment his eyes fell on the statuesque goddess. The woman was only a couple of inches shorter than Valentin but towered over Alex.

Her dark chocolate eyes assessed the two men immediately. '*Hmm, looking good but not good enough to look twice,*' Alina thought, and an amused light glimmered in her eyes.

'I wonder what she sees when she looks at us,' Alex wondered. *'Nothing flattering, I think,'* he frowned slightly. But then, the man waved his hand, inviting her wordlessly to take a seat in one of the available chairs around the table.

The two Police Inspectors waited for the woman to lower herself on the chair she chose. Their eyes fixated on her long legs, well showcased by the snug black pants and tall boots.

"I understand that one of our people was found dead in the elevator," she chirped in a melodic tone of voice, and for a few moments, both men watched with fascination how her full lips moved, forming words.

Then Alex shook off his bewitchment with the beautiful specimen before his eyes. *'Shake it off, man. You're not a damn schoolboy, and you have more pressing issues than looking stupid and spellbound.'*

"That is true," Alex confirmed, nodding sagely. "I understand you had a relationship with the man, besides your work connection," he specified, looking at her meaningfully.

The young woman smiled quizzically, and her smile lit her eyes, turning their dark chocolate color into molten onyx.

"Anything wrong with the question?" Alex arched his brow with dismay. The woman started to irritate him.

Alina's smile widened for a couple of seconds, and then the woman shook her head.

"No, nothing wrong, of course," she replied, shaking her head slightly. "Yes, you can say that we shared some personal moments together once upon the time."

"I see," Alex said, measuring the woman more attentively. She seemed too detached for a woman who had just found out that her former lover passed away. "Should I understand that no feelings were actually involved?" he lifted a brow quizzically.

The young woman's lips twitched. An ironic light lit her eyes, and she shrugged negligently. "I wouldn't say there was any love lost between the two of us, Police Inspector," Alina replied. "We both knew how things were between us, of course. I knew Dan wasn't the man to go steady, and he knew that I agreed wholeheartedly with a brief fling. I know he didn't expect that I would be the one ending the brief relationship, but then he didn't know me at all. I can confess that my pride wouldn't have taken it well if I waited for him to give me the leaving papers, so to speak. So, when I felt that things waned, I preferred to be the first who said *good bye*," Alina lifted one shoulder with indifference.

"So it was mostly like a race, to see which one of you would reach the finish line first," Valentin intervened.

"Something like that, if you want," the woman replied in an indifferent tone of voice.

"Any resentments?" Alex inquired.

"Why?" Alina arched her eyebrows. "It wasn't as if we hadn't had set limits from the beginning. Dan wanted the same thing, as well. What would have been the point for resentments? We both had fun while we were together. We stayed a sort of friends, I could say," she shrugged once more.

"I see. Is there anything that you could tell us about him?" Valentin asked, leaning forward.

"I suppose you've already heard everything that there was. Dan liked a variety of women. He got bored very easily and led a... let's say, reckless life," the woman reiterated the other people's words. "Maybe, he had some redeeming qualities," she pursed her lips, and her face showed that she was looking for an example "He had a good heart, I suppose," the young woman shrugged.

"You were his supervisor, I think," Alex intervened when he noticed that the woman didn't intend to add anything to that assessment.

"Not really," Alina smiled. "Because of our past relationship, Dan was moved to Lucien's team," she said, and the two men didn't fail to notice her pleasure to squash their suppositions.

"But you still have an idea about his overall performance and so on," Valentin insisted.

"He was all right, I suppose," Alina conceded. "I can't say he was very hardworking, but he did his job. I know he was permanently late, and Lucien was already sick of reprimanding him on a daily basis... But that was Dan, what can I say," the woman concluded, and a whimsical smile curved her lips.

"Do you know of any discussions between Dan and his colleagues or any problems?"

Alina burst into laughter and shook her head.

"What's so funny?" Valentin asked with puzzlement.

"Your question, I'm sorry," she replied. "Every single day, there was at least one person on the floor who had some bone to pick with him... Dan had a strange type of humor if you want, and he rubbed people the wrong way."

"Ah, I see," Alex nodded. "So that was the garden-variety squabble. What about something more serious? I mean something that went beyond a few words," he waved his hand.

"I think there were two or three. For instance, Samir. The other day, Samir exploded because Dan replaced his sandwich with a similar one. The problem was that the new sandwich was with pork instead of chicken. Imagine that it didn't go very well. Samir's religion doesn't allow him to eat pork, and the man is very attentive with such things. The two of them almost came to blows on the floor, and Lucien had to intervene. Lucien told Dan that he should reflect better before making such pranks because he couldn't mess just with everything."

"And in the end, how did things evolve?" Valentin asked, his eyes wide.

"I didn't hear any other discussions, but Dan and Samir stopped talking to each other. Samir is easy-going and mostly a very nice guy. Still, the man didn't find it in his soul to forgive Dan for that stupid prank," Alina lifted her right shoulder again. "That doesn't mean that I would see him in the role of a killer. Samir isn't built that way," she shook her head.

"Do you know where Samir was between twelve thirty and one thirty in the afternoon, let's say?" Alex asked her.

"Wow, that is quite the interval, I think," Alina laughed with surprise. "Still, he was on the floor," she assured them. "He came in late, again," the young woman mentioned with a brief giggle. "About an hour late, I could add," she shook her head. "He wouldn't have been able to leave before a quarter to two, the soonest, anyway."

"All right then. And the others you mentioned?" Alex insisted.

"There was Olivier, I think. A group of ten or fifteen guys went out for drinks one evening after work and drank for about five or six hours. I understand that when it came to paying the bill, Olivier decided to make himself scarce, but Dan intervened. Apparently, it wasn't the first time something like that happened, and Dan had had enough of that. They quarreled right there in the restaurant, and then we were *lucky* enough to hear discussions and veiled insults from one or the other for about a week now, I think," the woman explained and crossed her arms over her chest, leaning backward in her chair.

"Enough to lead to murder?" Valentin thought to inquire although he didn't believe it. All the same, people killed for the pettiest things.

"Not in my opinion," Alina shook her head with determination. "I have a hard time seeing Olivier do anything like that. He might have done something in the heat of the moment, but otherwise, he just grumbles."

"Still, where was he during the interval I mentioned?" Alex insisted.

"I can't say. He should have started work at one, I think. I'm pretty sure he's on the floor, she said, and then she stood up and moseyed toward the glass wall. She checked the floor intently, and then turned to them, "Yes, he's there. I spotted him," the woman specified and then tormented the men with the view of her long legs slowly moving back toward the table where she sat down with a graceful move.

"You said that there were about two or three people who had a bone to pick with Dan, I think," Alex intervened after he cleared his throat.

Alina grinned knowingly and crossed her legs.

"Yes, there's also Cristian," Alina nodded. "I am a bit reluctant to mention him because this one has actually had a fall out with everyone, including me," she waved her fingers and rolled her eyes with exasperation.

"How come?" Valentin asked with bewilderment.

"He's... a little special, let's say. The man either looks at you with contempt, as if you are a roach, good enough to squash you underneath the sole of his shoe, or with deep envy and implicitly with hatred. I don't believe he has made friends with anyone on the floor since he got hired, and it's been quite a while. I don't think anyone misses his friendship though," Alina made a grimace. "Moreover, he never has a good word about anyone," she shrugged.

"What happened between him and Dan?" Alex asked, looking at Alina intently, intrigued by the successive expressions on her face.

"Well, right before Dan started going out with Liza, Cristian tried his luck too, but Liza turned him down," Alina said with a wide wave of her hand. "Bad move for him," she shook her head. "I don't understand where he got the idea that he could get lucky. Anyway, from what I heard, Liza was unexpectedly nice. She just told Cristian that she didn't date people from the office. Then, she went out with Dan. Cristian had a few days of furious mumbling to himself. He threw dirty looks to the both of them, and even tried to come to me with imaginary mistakes one of them had made, requesting that I do something. When I didn't do anything, he went to the manager and complained of my lack of competence. Of course, the manager backed me, and as a result, the guy took an absence of leave for a few days. He was foaming at the mouth.

Literally," she told them in earnest, and her eyes rounded. "That did raise a few eyebrows around but no one is willing to fire a guy just because he's foaming. Even though, a few mentioned rabies, if I remember correctly," she smiled with a faraway look in her eyes. "That would have been a good excuse, but we would have needed to back it up with medical proof unfortunately," she grimaced.

"And when Cristian came back from his absence of leave what happened between the two of them?" Valentin asked impatiently. He felt on edge and couldn't wait to hear the conclusion of Alina's account.

"For a couple of weeks, he seemed all right. We concluded that he went back on his medication. Not that we know for sure that he was on a specific medication. Don't take me wrong," she hastened to explain. "It was just talk, you know."

The men nodded in a rush to make the woman continue, and Alina smiled. She liked it whenever she had a fascinated audience.

"Anyway, then Dan split with Liza. Cristian thought that it was his turn, but Liza merely said *no way*," she imparted that tidbit in a lower tone of voice. "The guy couldn't believe it and asked for explanations, right here on the floor," she continued with disbelief. Afterward, she tilted her head to the right and said, "If I think about it, it's like in a damn telenovela around here sometimes."

Her words prompted the officers to smile. The men had already reached the same conclusion, but they didn't expect her to say it.

"Anyway, when Cristian pointed out that she shouldn't be so smug because she had just been thrown aside by a damn womanizer, Liza told him that he wasn't good enough to wipe Dan's shoes, and he should wear a paper bag over his head. I'm pretty sure that you can imagine that that didn't go too well. Cristian has been looking at them with hatred ever since," Alina finally concluded her story.

"When did it happen?" Alex questioned.

"At the beginning of the week," Alina replied, and suddenly her phone beeped. The woman took it out and read the message, then she shifted her eyes toward the two policemen. "I'm needed on the floor. I'm sorry, but I do have to leave. If you have more questions, it will have to be another time," she said with regret.

"One last thing, before you go. Where was Cristian during that interval we mentioned?" Valentin hurried to ask.

"He's off today so I can't tell you," Alina shook her head. "I do need to go now. I must take a call," she said with an impatient gesture.

"I think we have everything we need," Alex said. "Maybe we could talk to that Samir now," he asked.

"Not a problem," Alina replied standing up, followed immediately by the officers. "If he's not in a call, I will send him to you. If he is, you'll have to wait for a while," she shrugged.

"If he is busy, maybe you can send that Olivier or the other supervisor, Lucien," Alex proposed. "We'd like to have a word with him as well, considering that he was Dan's direct supervisor."

"I'm afraid Lucien is not available at the hour," Alina shook her head, one hand on the door knob. "He doesn't work today," she explained. "You can come back tomorrow if you want. But then, I can send Olivier to you if Samir is on a call. Let's only hope that they aren't both busy at the same time," she laughed merrily, the subject of their discussion already forgotten. The woman threw her thick mane over her shoulder, and left the room with supple steps.

The two men's eyes followed her exist with disbelief.

"That's one hard nut to crack," Valentin observed, and Alex nodded curtly, turning his eyes to the notes he had scribbled in his little book.

CHAPTER FOURTEEN

Alex and Valentin got into the elevator and Alex pushed the ground floor key. They were both tired to the bones. It was already past eight in the evening, and the officers had talked to several people by then.

"What do you think about a drink?" Alex proposed suddenly, and his invitation prompted Valentin's eyebrows to shot up.

The officer had never invited anyone from the headquarters to a beer or a coffee. Everyone knew that Alex didn't like to mingle with his colleagues and didn't socialize.

Alex observed his colleague's bewilderment and grinned. Then, he thought to be more precise, so he added, "It wasn't an invitation to have a heart to heart discussion. I merely thought to ease the stress a little. Of course, if you don't have anything else to do," he mentioned, while passing by Camelia, Popa's last conquest. '*I wonder where Popa is now, and how he fared,*' Alex reflected pensively.

"I'm free until ten," Valentin finally answered, making Alex turn his eyes toward him.

"What happens at ten?" Alex asked once they cleared the turning door and got in front of the building.

The cool evening air filled his lungs, together with the smog. The smell of overused tires invaded his nostrils, and Alex grimaced. As Valentin didn't answer, Alex shifted his eyes to him, and his right eyebrow arched. Valentin had turned scarlet and was biting his lips.

"Is there something wrong?" Alex inquired, arching an eyebrow with curiosity.

"Not really," the man said in a weak tone of voice.

Alex studied Valentin's face with curiosity for a few moments, and then the truth dawned on him. With a barely concealed grin, he observed, "I suppose you arranged for a date with Carmen," he observed negligently and had the satisfaction to see his colleague get more flustered.

'*A man must find his fun where he can,*' he mused, not feeling guilty because of that.

Alex laughed and thumped Valentin on the back. "Good for you. So I suppose that you have time for a beer," Alex surmised. "That is until ten o'clock, I mean," he thought to specify.

Valentin nodded, although he didn't feel very confident that Alex wouldn't make fun of him. Moreover, he didn't know for sure if he was supposed not to make friends with the people he interviewed.

'*Anyway, it is too late to question that,*' the young Police Inspector concluded and fell in step with Alex.

The two men strode lazily along the street, just breathing in the evening air. Alex shoved his hands in his pockets, whistling softly under his beard.

"Do you know what I don't get?" Valentin suddenly said, and Alex turned his head to him with puzzlement. The man had already plunged deeply in his thoughts.

"What's that?" Alex felt compelled to ask.

"How did the killer know that no one would be on the third floor when he or she waited there to kill Dan? I also don't know how a man or a woman covered in blood could have crossed Bucharest without raising questions," Valentin said, waving his hand with agitation.

"Ah, that," Alex replied softly. "I talked to one of the guys from Dan's team. You know, when we split to cover the interviews faster," Alex reminded to him, and Valentin nodded. "Well, it seems that the third floor has a terrace, and people from there don't go downstairs to smoke. Plus, people on that floor usually start going to lunch after one thirty, but mostly after two or two thirty. So, I suppose that the killer knew that," Alex shrugged. "About the blood thing... I doubt the murderer crossed the town covered in blood," he shook his head. "It wouldn't have been possible, of course. Either the guy or the woman – because it might have been a woman, wore something like a raincoat or they had clothes to change, which I really doubt," Alex shook his head once more, and his lips became a thin line.

CHAPTER FOURTEEN

When he stepped into the corridor leading to his office, Alex stopped shortly. Popa leaned on a wall, disheveled and with circles under his eyes. The man looked as if he had been through several sleepless nights.

"Morning," Alex greeted the Police Sub-Inspector. "Have you slept?" he wondered.

The man just waved his question away, as if it hadn't been important, but then he said, "I wouldn't say no to some coffee, if you're offering one."

Alex grinned and waved to the man to follow him. Popa fell in step with the Inspector, stifling a huge yawn. It was clear that the man moved only through sheer will.

Alex led the Sub-Inspector to his office and invited him to take a seat while he started preparing the coffee.

He busied himself with measuring the ground coffee into the coffee maker and then turned toward Popa who remained standing next to the Alex's desk.

"Any news?" Alex asked the man who seemed to be sleeping still standing. *'He definitely didn't get any rest last night,'* the young man concluded.

"Don't I always come through?" Popa wondered, arching an eyebrow haughtily.

"So?" the Inspector also arched his right brow, as it was his habit.

The Sub-Inspector grinned seeing that characteristic gesture, and then he ruffled his hair with the tips of his fingers.

"I found Geo last night in a village at about fifty miles from Bucharest. Of course, I had a little talk with him. If you're interested, the man is in one of the interrogation rooms right now. He's writing his statement under a uniformed policeman's vigilant eyes," the short man joked and eyed the coffee maker expectantly.

"It will be ready in a minute," Alex reassured Popa when he observed the direction of the man's gaze. "What did Geo say?" he tried to make the Sub-Inspector get back to the point of their conversation.

"Well, it's like in those novels with spies and conspiracies," the swarthy man winked, and Alex's lips turned upward.

'This man always is able to make me smile. Even so early in the morning,' Alex reflected with wonder.

The Inspector had drunk one beer too many the previous night and didn't feel quite as well as always.

"Could you develop this idea a bit?" Alex Pop waved at the man to nudge him to talk.

"Not really," the Sub-Inspector shook his head, and his eyes turned stubborn. "First, give me my coffee," he pointed out with steel determination in his voice, making Alex laugh.

"You'll get it right now," Alex said, shaking his head with amusement.

Luckily, the coffee maker just announced the completion of the brewing process, so Alex grabbed two cups and poured the potent liquid up to the rim of the mugs.

"You know I don't keep any sugar or milk around," he warned the Sub-Inspector.

The man just waved his hand dismissively and snatched the cup out of the Inspector's hand. He sipped carefully a couple of times, and then, satisfied, he sat down in one of the chairs before Alex's desk.

"That Geo told me everything he knew," Popa started talking after he sipped from his mug once more. "You only have to parade the right man before his eyes, and Geo would be able to point directly at the murderer," he said.

CHAPTER FIFTEEN

"So, I heard you two solved your case," Police Chief-Commissioner Baranga said, waving to the two Inspectors to take a seat.

Alex shifted his eyes to the people in attendance, and then, he shrugged. He didn't know if he was in for another scolding at the end, but it didn't really matter. They did solve the case or at least contributed to that.

"Actually, sir, I think that Police Sub-Inspector Popa solved the case," Alex decided to be honest. "He found Geo, the security guard, and that one gave us all the information we needed to close the case," he explained.

"I haven't read the report yet," the Chief-Commissioner replied. "I'd prefer to hear from you how everything fell into place."

Alex shrugged but continued.

"Well, Cristian effectively lost his mind over that Liza story. I'm saying that he did lose his mind because he was well on his way there before that. We checked, and the man has been on medication all his entire life. I think his mother is to blame, but... Anyway, I am not a psychologist so I won't go down that road," he surmised.

"But how did he pull it off?" Baranga asked, folding his hands on the desk.

"First, he managed to charm one of the cleaning ladies. Don't ask me how," he put up his hand. "Because it seemed unbelievable. And yet, he did it. Probably she was taken away with his diplomas – he has about three or four degrees, I think. Anyway, after a few dates, he convinced her to find Geo's phone number. He heard the security guard talking over the phone a few times and found out that the guy was well over his head in debt. Geo likes to bet. A lot."

"So he offered money to the man," the Chief-Commissioner surmised.

"Not so simple," Alex shook his head. "Cristian created a very convoluted story. He called the guard with a private number and promised to give him ten thousand lei if he just let him know when a certain person would get onto an elevator. Then, Geo was supposed to go into the office in the back for a few minutes. He told the guard that he wanted to pull a prank which involved some splattering of Dan's clothes with something, and it would have been better if the guard didn't see it. Thus, he wouldn't have had to lie if he was asked anything. When the guard proved skeptic, he promised five thousand more, but with the condition that Geo would also turn off the camera on the third floor. We checked. Cristian took a fifteen thousand lei loan, a week before. The money was delivered by courier to the front desk for Geo."

"So, did that Geo do what he was told?" Baranga inquired.

"In a way," Valentin whispered.

"Speak up, man," the Chief-Commissioner thundered, and Alex grinned, lowering his head so that no one could see his face.

"Geo took the money, sir. He called Cristian to let him know when Dan went upstairs. But he didn't turn the camera off immediately and saw Cristian waiting on the third floor. The guy wore a raincoat. Then, the security guard stopped the recording, not knowing what would happen next."

"Well, at least he was able to identify the killer," the Police Chief-Commissioner concluded. "Have you arrested the murderer already?" the man inquired.

The two Police Inspectors nodded, and the prosecutor smiled, shaking his head.

"It was a serious circus when we arrested Cristian, but we did arrest him," Alex said with a brief nod. "Geo's also arrested, by the way," he mentioned.

"I would have thought so," the Police Chief-Commissioner said in a dry tone of voice. "All right, leave the report with me and you are off for the day," Baranga said in a hard tone of voice, although his eyes showed his satisfaction. '*They're good even though not seasoned yet,*' he reflected.

The two young men hurried out of the office immediately. Baranga's company didn't attract them too much given any time of the day.

"Any plans for today?" Alex turned to Valentin.

"A hot date with Carmen," this one winked at his colleague. "You?"

Alex sighed, looked away for a few seconds, but then the man confessed, "I got a date too, with Ana-Maria, but I am not very sure in what I got myself into," he confessed.

Valentin laughed while descending the stairs to the street. The wind ruffled his hair, and the man felt again like a naughty teenager, rushing out to date a girl.

Alex grinned and shook his head. '*Not bad, this Valentin, at all,*' he concluded.

EXCERPT FROM THE NOVEL A SUITABLE EPITAPH

PROLOGUE – AXEL'S VISION

THE WOMAN HAD BEEN flirting with him for over fifteen minutes before he invited her to accompany him in the garden for some fresh air. Glancing out the patio doors into the darkness, she smiled. That was exactly what she'd been aiming for and she consented freely to follow him outside.

After all he was a very well built man. Maybe quite too well, she thought when she noticed him for the first time. Her mouth watered while her eyes perused the expanse of his broad shoulders and strong hands.

She needed a man. It had been some time since a man's strong hands aroused her. Probably, too long, if she considered the flutter in her belly.

The physical desire had been compelling enough, but the signs hinting to his wealth had been more important and decisive for her. The man was wealthy enough for her tastes. His suit wasn't a cheap imitation but a true Armani. She'd always had an eye for such things.

They strolled leisurely along the gravel path as she clung to his sturdy arm. He murmured some inconsequential things and she didn't bother to listen.

The power she could feel under her fingers was as exciting as the heavy smell of the roses lining the one side of the trail. She smelled romance in the air and smiled.

A few more steps and the roses made way to berry bushes. The smells changed and the heat of the summer night enveloped them in a humid cocoon.

THE MAN IN THE ELEVATOR

The shingle path disappeared and she stumbled when her foot stepped on cracked soil. Both chuckled although embarrassment powdered her cheeks with a slight blush. He silently provided more support to her and a giddy feeling bubbled in her veins.

When he hastened his steps, she giggled softly and commented playfully on his haste. He was watching the trees, distracted, and didn't give any sign that he'd heard.

That determined her to bring a halt to their fast advancement through the garden. It might have been romantic, yet it didn't seem very wise. She was alone with a man she'd just met and didn't know anything about him.

It was her first time there and she hadn't been aware that the garden grounds were so extensive and secluded. Besides, while she had all intentions to flirt with him, she didn't have any intentions to succumb to his charms that night.

It was never a good idea to give in too soon. She wanted much more than a tumble in the hay and that meant that she had to play hard to get for a while. Men liked the hunt. They enjoyed the scent of their prey and the efforts that came with their chase.

The huge man glanced at her. His eyes showed understanding and he allowed her to move at a slower pace. She was wearing stilettoes and her feet thanked him. When she put on her high heels that evening before the party, she hadn't meant to wear them on that hard ground.

Once they were about forty meters away from the house and in the shadow of the trees lining that side of the garden, the man grabbed her arm and nudged her to a deserted corner. He put enough strength behind his action and the brutal move startled her.

A shiver played on the back of her neck and sent tentacles along her spine and the back of her legs. A spine-chilling feeling replaced her light-hearted mood from before, but she didn't take it lying down.

She tried to reason with him at first. She preferred to assume that maybe he was too anxious to be alone with her and that was why his attitude changed. Her well-chosen words fell on deaf ears though, and she stopped pretending. She began to oppose him but it was as if she'd been trying to stop a river flow.

Indifferent to her pleas, he dragged her for a few more meters. She continued pleading with him because she didn't see any other solution, but her attempts failed. She replenished her efforts to fight him and tried to dig her heels in the ground, but the soil was too dry and she couldn't get any traction. She just stirred a cloud of dust that rushed to find a home in her pores.

Her legs turned to jelly and she barely kept herself upright. Something was definitely wrong with what was going on there. Both her self-confidence and sense of safety had slowly skulked away during the forced walk through the trees.

Tinges of electrical shocks ran through her arms. She panicked and tears burnt her cheeks. She felt ashamed of her weakness and tried to hold them back, but the cold fingers of fear kept squeezing her heart in an iron fist, and her breath became ragged.

THE MAN IN THE ELEVATOR

Probably sick of her puny attempts to detangle herself from him, he finally stopped and moved to stand before her. Through the stream of her stubborn tears she surveyed the man's stony face with dread. The man wasn't even blinking and that disconcerted her more. He was just staring at her with dead eyes which quashed her hopes.

She tried to say something again, but now she didn't find the strength to push the sounds past her lips. Her throat refused to work and her mouth was drier than the soil she felt under the thin soles of her fancy shoes.

She glanced back to the house with renewed albeit premature expectation but the trees hid it from sight. Her lips quaked when she realized that no one could see or hear her.

A corner of the man's mouth lifted in a satisfied smirk, and that sneer was a splash of cold water over her face. Even though her anxiety was climbing and reaching new heights, she understood that what he felt for her was nothing else but contempt.

That came like a shock. Not the first that evening to be sure, but this one packed the power of a live wire and her mind scattered looking for an explanation.

She'd always been certain that men admired and even worshipped her. She'd basked in their burning glances often enough and she knew that she didn't delude herself.

She stared back at him with tired eyes. She tried to decipher what lay there behind the mask but her intuition had taken cover somewhere and didn't offer any help.

The sturdy man studied her for a few moments and then, he reached out and fisted his hand over her silk blouse. His touch brought her back to the reality which had twisted a pretend romance into a horror movie. Fear bubbled near the surface now and, as her brain scrambled the signals, she was about to burst into a hysterical laughter.

In that frozen moment, that soft blouse which caressed the curve of her breasts became the most important thing in her world. She was very proud of that top as it was one of the symbols she attached to the life she'd built for herself. She'd turned that expensive piece of silk into a tangible proof that she'd exceeded both her and other people's expectations but, more important, that she'd escaped her birth circumstances, which had confined her to the working class.

The sight of that dark and threatening hand on her precious top brought a glimmer of dread but also made her see red before her eyes.

The beefy hand jerked hard and the flimsy blouse fell apart rendered to rags. Her dismay and the pressure of her fury at the sight of her prized chemise ruined ruthlessly, pushed a warlike cry past her quivering lips.

She abandoned any rational thought and jumped the man. Her shoes found soft spots in his shins and made him grunt. Her nails targeted the handsome and ruthless face she'd admired just minutes before and left blood in their wake.

He fought her back. The slap of his backhand unbalanced her. She stumbled back and cried out again and not only because of the pain. This cry echoed the terror that had swiftly creeped into her bones and fried all her neuronal cells. The man was strong and she didn't have the ability to defend herself against that brutal show of force.

Her cry died soon, though. Another man grabbed her throat from behind and his fingers gripped her as a vise and smothered the sound.

She questioned and berated herself. In the heat of the fight she'd failed to hear the other man's steps. Still, she promised herself to go down swinging.

She tried to claw into his skin but he didn't show that he registered any kind of pain. Running on instinct only, she directed her stilettoes to his shins but she couldn't say for sure if she succeeded. His fingers burrowed harder into the delicate skin and left bruises behind that marred the flawless whiteness of her epidermis. Her air pipe constricted and the woman slid slowly into unconsciousness.

Before she blacked out, she had just enough time to feel other fingers knotted in her hair. She was beyond terror and anxiety. Her impotence overwhelmed the solitary corner of her mind that was still functioning. The last thought that passed her mind was that she couldn't buy or fight her way out of that. She'd lost the game and that was her night.

The slight flicker of life in her body just made it interesting for the men around. The third man who'd grabbed her hair, threw her on the hard ground in the shadow of a bush pregnant with red drops. Her skirt climbed up and the whiteness of the exposed skin of her legs lit the darkness.

The three of them were still looming over her. They stared at her fallen body for a few seconds.

One of the attackers smirked with satisfaction, his eyes going from her body to the red berries. The ugliness in his sneer showed that he knew that the beauty of the red fruit went hand in hand with their poison and he found it befitting the situation. The woman was about to get what she deserved. Poison deserved poison.

Axel woke up with a jerk and his half-lidded eyes surveyed the bedroom. The light of the moon reflected in the glass panels of the south wall and filled the room with shadows in the corners.

His heart pounded in his chest. For one brief but agonizing moment, he'd feared that he was there with those men, who were still staring at the woman's body, which was lying in the shadow of that bush.

Now, wide awake, he breathed deeply and closed his eyes in relief. He was still in his house.

Axel's relief was short lived. He'd scarcely closed his eyes, that he had another vision of the woman's broken body.

She was lying down on that hard and dry ground which he'd seen in his dream. Now, a monotonous rain whipped her mercilessly and washed the pattern in blood which had been painted on her body, feeding it to the dehydrated soil.

The vision was so in-depth that Axel could even see the rain drops clinging to the woman's eyelashes. The light in her eyes had dimmed at first and then vanished. The lines on her forehead had deepened and marked her passing years on her face.

A few hours earlier, that face had been flawless. Now it was marred with an x high on her left cheekbone and her features showed weariness, pain and despair.

Axel flexed his fingers and wiped his damp palms off on his thighs. Axel's visions weren't always so detailed, but there were exceptions, such as the one that he'd had that night.

THE MAN IN THE ELEVATOR

When the image finally blurred, Axel exhaled in a whoosh and then breathed in deeply. He wiped his forehead and noticed that his fingers weren't as steady as he knew them.

Axel shook his head and got off his bed and tried to stand. He had to lean on the night table for a few seconds before trying his wobbly legs again.

In the usual course of events, the man wouldn't have needed help to find his bearings. Axel knew his lair as well as the back of his hand and could find his way through the rooms even if he hadn't pulled the curtains aside to have the room bathed in the light of the moon. Still, that night, he needed the support of the walls to reach the bathroom.

There, he leaned on the lavabo and stared at his reflection in the mirror. Staring didn't help though. He turned on the tap and filled his fists with cold water which he liberally splashed over his face.

When the trepidation had left his body, Axel drank a mouthful. His mouth had been dry and his tongue was almost stuck to the roof of the mouth.

It wasn't enough. He brushed his teeth and only then he left the bathroom. He started towards his terrace but hesitated. He was restive and needed something more than to just listen to the owls in the night and the sounds of the lake.

With a shrug, he turned around and left his bedroom. He needed a glass of his best whiskey to wash away the metallic taste of death which still lingered in his mouth. His toothpaste hadn't succeeded in chasing it away. He also needed to make a decision.

Axel didn't know the people in his dream, but he knew the house. He'd seen that garden before. He'd strolled around it many times in the past and knew exactly where to find that pregnant bush.

Now, he had to decide what to say to the police and how. He didn't want to reveal how he knew about the crime but they would ask and he needed to plot a strategy.

THE MAN IN THE ELEVATOR

EXCERPT FROM THE NOVEL
AN IMMIGRANT

The echo of hasty steps coming from the direction of the Gigue reached his ears. With trepidation, Victor lifted his head and stared unblinkingly into the night.

Anxiety and fear nudged at him and he pushed hard with his palms into the ground to move. Pain instantly radiated everywhere in his back, but resolute, gritting his teeth, he tried to crawl under a tree. It felt as if he had moved through molasses. Each inch he covered brought more sweat and aches.

'*At least I'm alive,*' Victor thought. '*But not for long, if I don't move out of this darn trail,*' he groused and pushed harder, gritting his teeth to contain his grunts.

"He fell somewhere here," a strong male voice shredded the silence.

"Are you sure? I can't see anyone," a throaty female voice replied with evident doubt.

Victor stopped any movement and tried to become one with the ground. He knew he was in the shadow and they couldn't see him.

"I can hear him," the woman said with enthusiasm, and Victor grimaced.

'*How the heck can you hear me?*' he wondered and his eyes widened. His fingers dug into the floor of the grove, as if he wanted to anchor himself.

'*I'm not saying jack,*' he thought. '*I'm not so out of my mind that I'm talking without being aware of that, aren't I?*'

"Yeah, I hear him too," the man's voice replied. "He's kept his humor so he mustn't be in a very bad shape," he noticed drily.

Victor's eyebrows shot up his forehead. *'Who the heck are these people? More important, what the heck do they want with me?'*

"I don't hear anyone around," the woman said. "Take out your flashlight," she ordered.

'She's like a drill sergeant,' Victor mused, listening intently to every sound they made.

VICTOR GAVE UP ANY pretense when the light swept over him. He didn't know those people but there were only two options —either they came to save him or finish him. There wasn't any way around that.

He lifted his head, and gnashing his teeth, he turned to the light. The flashlight blinded him, and this time, he couldn't hold a groan.

"He's there," the man said, and rushed to kneel next to Victor. "Hey, buddy, are you still with us?" he asked, and Victor sensed the smile in his voice.

Victor grunted and nodded once. He didn't know whether he still had his voice. His eyes searched the man's face. Satisfied he had never seen him before, he laid his head on his folded arms again, and closed his eyes.

"Is he still alive?" the woman's voice asked.

"Yes, he is. What should we do now?" the man inquired, rousing Victor's curiosity.

'Why would he ask for her advice?' he thought, and the next moment, the man's laughter filled the air.

"Because she's the boss now," the man replied with good humor.

His words shocked Victor, and he just froze, his eyes zeroed in on Axel. He couldn't even blink.

"Now look what you've done, Axel," the woman chided her companion. "You scared him."

"He'll survive," Axel answered matter-of-factly, and Victor had the distinct impression that the man shrugged with nonchalance.

"Who are you people?" Victor croaked, unable to keep his mouth shut one second more.

He felt as if he had fallen in a strange dimension. This time, he was sure he hadn't voiced his question.

The woman's cold hand brushed his hair off his forehead, soothing his increasing fever.

"I'm Leah MacKay, a detective, and this is my boyfriend, Axel Arnett," she replied in a kind voice. "I'm going to call an ambulance for you," she continued.

She tried to stand up but the man's fingers closed over her wrist with surprising strength.

"No police," he groused.

He bit his lips. The sudden move had sparked arrows of pain along his spine and lower body.

Arnett burst into a hearty laughter. The sound gritted on Victor's nerves. If he had had the strength, he would have knocked the man down.

"Sorry, pal, the police are already here," Axel explained with cheer, making Victor lock his teeth again.

THE MAN IN THE ELEVATOR

Leah pried his fingers off her wrist gently and took her cell phone out of her pocket. She dialed 911 and explained to the operator who she was and that she needed an ambulance and her team at the Sarabande.

Defeated, Victor sighed and laid his head on his arms again. He'd seen a commercial once with a small hedgehog coming out of a hole just to be hammered down once more. Now, he was the hedgehog. He had lost control of his life. '*Eh, it's not for the first time,*' he mused.

Axel Arnett leaned over him and whispered, "Everything will be well, don't worry. She's the best."

"That's what I'm afraid of," Victor grumbled, prompting Axel to chuckle.

Axel liked the man and felt satisfaction that they got to him in time. Hopefully, he would survive.

Axel felt the strength in him and counted on his built. He wasn't a man that could be easily taken down.

AUTHOR'S BIOGRAPHY

BORN IN EUROPE, SOME time ago, the writer started loving books very early and the next step was easy: writing became a dream and a purpose.

She enjoys writing and baking - these two work very well hand in hand, and she enjoys spending time with her dog - or at least most of the time, as he is a hellion.

One trip to Scotland made her lose her heart to a beautiful country and extraordinary people and that is why she chose a Scottish detective to promote most of her crime stories.

THE MAN IN THE ELEVATOR

BOOKS BY ROXANA NASTASE

Mayhem on Nightingale Street – McNamara Series – Book One

Scents and Shadows – McNamara Series – Book Two

McNamara Series – Box Set (Book One – Mayhem on Nightingale Street & Scents and Shadows)

A Suitable Epitaph – MacKay - Canadian Detectives Series - Book One

An Immigrant – MacKay - Canadian Detectives Series – Book Two

MacKay - Canadian Detectives Series – Book Set (A Suitable Epitaph & An Immigrant)

A Churchgoing Woman

Relative Bonds

Payback Is a Bitch

FORTHCOMING:

A Change of Heart – MacKay - Canadian Detectives Series – Book Three

Don't miss out!

Visit the website below and you can sign up to receive emails whenever Roxana Nastase publishes a new book. There's no charge and no obligation.

https://books2read.com/r/B-A-QVJD-QEDW

BOOKS 2 READ

Connecting independent readers to independent writers.

Did you love *The Man in the Elevator*? Then you should read *MacKay - Canadian Detectives Series Book One*[1] by Roxana Nastase!

[2]

Canadian Detectives, part of the police force or private investigators, are in pursuit of truth and justice. They navigate the twists and ugliness of their cases and in the end, they get more than they bargained for – they also lose their hearts.

A Suitable Epitaph introduces the Canadian Lieutenant Leah Mackay and her team while solving the case of Klavdiya's murder. Klavdiya dreamed of money and love. Her dreams died with her under a merciless rain. Leah, a Canadian detective

1. https://books2read.com/u/bpW7XW

2. https://books2read.com/u/bpW7XW

with empathetic skills, and her team engage in a tedious race to find the culprit. Leah is able to read people's minds and sense their feelings and she makes good use of her skills. However, when she encounters Axel, her abilities are blocked and she doesn't know if she found her killer or merely a witness to the murder. If you like a detective story with compelling characters, then this is the book for you.

An Immigrant brings a private detective in the mist of the Canadian detectives. Victor is on the trail of soulless killers and ends up at the tip of a blade. Will he survive with his hide in one piece? 'An Immigrant' is a crime novel weaved with suspense, twists and turns, romance and dry humor now and then. It will intrigue and hook you. A touch of paranormal will sprinkle the story and raise the interest a notch. Don't miss your chance to delve into a convoluted intrigue and meet unique characters. Oh, and don't forget – you will get a bonus at the end of the novel – the recipe for one of the most delicious Romanian cakes. It melts in your mouth, with an explosion of flavors. Disclaimer: the taste matches the calories and it is addictive.

Read more at roxananastase.weebly.com.

About the Publisher

It is based in Toronto and brings to public various books: poems, novels, short-stories, children's books, language study books and non-fiction. It publishes the literary review: Scarlet Leaf Review: www.scarletleafreview.com

Our mission is to help emerging authors and poets to make their works known to the public.

Contact email address: scarletleafpublishinghouse@gmail.com

www.ingramcontent.com/pod-product-compliance
Lightning Source LLC
Chambersburg PA
CBHW060124260626
47160CB00005B/2008